CW00740881

The Rover Boys
In
The Air

Edward Stratemeyer

Copyright © 2023 Culturea Editions
Text and cover : © public domain
Edition : Culturea (Hérault, 34)
Contact : infos@culturea.fr
Print in Germany by Books on Demand
Design and layout : Derek Murphy
Layout : Reedsy (https://reedsy.com/)
ISBN : 9791041952564
Légal deposit : September 2023
All rights reserved

THE ROVER BOYS IN THE AIR

CHAPTER I

THE BOYS AND THE BIPLANE

"Fo' de land sakes, Massa Dick, wot am dat contraption yo' boys dun put togedder back ob de bahn yesterday?"

"Why, Aleck, don't you know what that is?" returned Dick Rover, with a smile at the colored man. "That's a biplane."

"A biplane, eh?" repeated Alexander Pop, the colored helper around the Rover homestead. He scratched his woolly head thoughtfully. "Yo' don't mean to say it am lak a plane a carpenter man uses, does yo', Massa Dick? 'Pears lak to me it was moah lak some ship sails layin' down,somethin' lak dem ships we see over in Africy, when we went into dem jungles to find yo' fadder."

"No, it has nothing to do with a carpenter's plane, Aleck," answered Dick, with a laugh. "A biplane is a certain kind of a flying machine."

"Wat's dat? A flyin' machine? Shorely, Massa Dick, yo' ain't gwine to try to fly?" exclaimed Aleck, in horror.

"That is just what I am going to do, Aleck, after I have had a few lessons. I hope to fly right over the house, just like a bird."

"No! no! Don't you try dat, Massa Dick! You'll break yo' neck suah! Don't yo' try it! II can't allow it nohowan' yo' aunt won't allow it neither!" And the colored man shook his head most emphatically.

"Now, don't get excited, Aleck," said Dick, calmly. "I won't go up until I am sure of what I am doing. Why, don't you know that flying in the air is getting to be a common thing these days? Tom and Sam and I bought that biplane in New York last week, and a man who knows all about flying is coming out to the farm to teach us how to run it. After we know how to sail through the air we'll take you up with us."

"Me!" ejaculated the colored man, and rolled his eyes wildly. "Not in a thousand years, Massa Dick, an' not fo' all dat treasure yo' dun brung home from Treasure Isle! No, sah, de ground am good enough fo' Aleck Pop!" And he backed away, as if afraid Dick Rover might carry him off then and there.

"Hello, Aleck!" cried a merry voice at this moment, and Tom Rover came into view. "Want to take a sail through the clouds for a change?"

"Massa Tom, am yo' really thinking ob goin' up in dat contraption?" demanded the colored man, earnestly.

"Sure thing, Aleck. And you'll want to go, too, before long. Think of flying along like a bird!" And Tom Rover spread out his arms and moved them slowly up and down. "Oh, it's grand!"

"Yo' won't be no bird when yo' come down kerflop!" murmured Aleck, soberly. "Yo' will be all busted up, dat's wot yo'll be!"

"We won't fall, don't you worry," continued Tom. "This biplane is a firstclass machine, warranted in all kinds of weather."

"If it am a flyin' machine wot fo' you call it a biplane?" asked the colored man curiously.

"Bi stands for two," explained Dick. "A bicycle means two cycles, or two wheels. A biplane means two planes, or two surfaces of canvas. This biplane of ours, as you can see, has two surfaces, or decks, an upper and a lower. A monoplane has only one plane, and a triplane has three. Now you understand, don't you, Aleck?"

"I dun reckon I do, Massa Dick. But look yeah, boys, yo' take my advice an' don't yo' try to sail frough de air in dat bicycleplane, or wot yo' call it. 'Tain't safe nohow! Yo' stick to de hosses, an' dat autermobile, an' de boat on de ribber. A boy wasn't meant to be a bird nohow!"

"How about being an angel, Aleck?" asked Tom, slyly.

"Huh! An angel, eh? Well, if yo' go up in dat bicycleplane maybe yo' will be an angel after yo' fall out, even if yo' ain't one when yo' starts." And with this remark Aleck Pop hurried away to his work in the house.

"That's one on you, Tom," cried Dick, with a broad smile. "Poor Aleck! he evidently has no use for flying machines."

"Well, Dick, now the machine is together, it does look rather scary," answered Tom Rover, slowly. "I want to see that aviator try it out pretty well before I risk my neck going up."

"Oh, so do I. And we'll have to have a good many lessons in running the engine, and in steering, and all that. I begin to think running a flying machine is a good deal harder than running an auto, or a motor boat."

"Yes, I guess it is. Come on down and let us see how the engine works. We can do that easily enough, for it's a good deal like the engine of an auto, or a motor boat," went on Tom.

"Where is Sam?"

"He took the auto and went down to the Corners on an errand for Aunt Martha. He said he'd be back as soon as possible. He's as crazy to get at the biplane as either of us."

The two boys walked to where the biplane had been put together, in a large open wagon shed attached to the rear of the big barn. The biplane has a stretch from side to side of over thirty feet, and the shed had been cleaned out from end to end to make room for it. There was a rudder in front and another behind, and in the centre was a broad cane seat, with a steering wheel, and several levers for controlling the craft. Back of the seat was the engine, lightly built but powerful, and above was a goodsized tank of gasoline. The framework of the biplane was of bamboo, held together by stays of piano wire, and the planes themselves were of canvas, especially prepared so as to be almost if not quite air proof. All told, the machine was a fine one, thoroughly uptodate, and had cost considerable money.

"We'll have to get a name for this machine," remarked Tom. "Have you any in mind?"

"Well, Ierthought we might call her theer" And then his big brother stopped short and grew slightly red in the face.

"I'll bet an apple you were going to say Dora," cried Tom quickly.

"Humph," murmured Dick. "Maybe you were going to suggest Nellie."

"No, I wasn't," returned Tom, and now he got a little red also. "If I did that, Sam might come along and want to name it the Grace. We had better give the girls' names a rest. Let's call her the Dartaway, that is, if she really does dart away when she flies."

4

"All right, Tom; that's a firstclass name," responded Dick. "And Dartaway she shall become, if Sam is willing. Now then, we'll fill that gasoline tank and let the engine warm up a bit. Probably it will need some adjusting."

"Can we use the same gasoline as we use in the auto?"

"Yes, on ordinary occasions. In a race you can use a higher grade, so that aviator said. But then you'll have to readjust the magneto and carburetor."

"Gracious, Dick! You're not thinking of an air race already, are you!"

"Oh, no! But we might get in a race some day,and such things are good to know," answered Dick, as he walked off to the garage, where there was a barrel of gasoline sunk in the ground, with a pipe connection. He got out a fivegallon can and filled it, and then poured the gasoline in the tank of the biplane.

"She'll hold more than that," said Tom, watching him. "Here, give me the can and I'll fill the tank while we are at it. We'll want plenty of gas when that aviator gets here."

In a few minutes more the gasoline tank was full, and then the two lads busied themselves putting the engine in running order, and in filling up the lubricating oil box. They also oiled up the working parts, and oiled the propeller bearings and the steering gear.

"Now, I guess she is all ready to run," remarked Dick, at length. "My, but isn't she a beauty, Tom! Just think of sailing around in her!"

"I'd like to go up right now!" answered the brother. "If only I knew more about airships, hang me if I wouldn't try it!"

"Don't you dream of it, yet!" answered Dick. "We've got to learn the art of it, just like a baby has got to learn to walk. If you went up now you'd come down with a smash sure."

"Maybe I would," mused Tom. "Well, let us try the engine anyhow. And maybe we can try the propellers," he added, with a longing glance at the smooth, wooden blades.

"One thing at a time," answered Dick, with a laugh. "We'll try the engine, but we'll have to tie the biplane fast, or else it may run into something and get smashed."

"Let us run her out into the field first. It's too gloomy in the shed. I'll hammer in some stakes and tie her."

The biplane rested on three small rubbertired wheels, placed in the form of a triangle. Thus it was an easy matter to roll the big machine from the shed to the level field beyond. Then Tom ran back and procured some stakes, several ropes, and a hammer, and soon he had the biplane staked fast to the ground, after the manner of a small circus tent.

"Now she can't break loose, even if you do start the engine and the propellers," said he, as he surveyed his work. "Go ahead, Dick, and turn on the juice!" he cried impatiently.

Dick Rover was just as anxious to see the engine work, and after another critical inspection he turned on the battery and then walked to one of the propellers.

"We'll have to start the engine by turning these," he said.

"All right!" cried Tom, catching hold of the other wooden blades. "Now then, all ready? Heave ahoy, my hearty!" he added, in sailor fashion.

Four times were the wooden blades "turned over" and still the engine refused to respond. It was hard work, and both of the lads perspired freely, for it was a hot day in early September.

"Got that spark connected all right?" panted Tom, as he stopped to catch his breath.

"Yes," was the reply, after Dick had made an inspection. "The engine is cold, that's all."

"Humph, well I'm not! But come on, let us give her another twist."

The brothers took hold again, and, at a word from Dick, each gave the wooden paddles of the propellers a vigorous turn. There came a sudden hiss, followed by a crack and a bang, and then off the engine started with the loudness of a gattling gun.

"Hurrah! she's started!" yelled Tom, triumphantly. "Say, but she makes some noise, doesn't she?" he added.

"I should say yes. That's because airship engines don't have mufflers, like autos," yelled back Dick, to make himself heard above the explosions.

"And see those propellers go around!" went on Tom, in deep admiration. "All you can see is a whirr! We sure have a dandy engine in this craft, Dick!"

"Looks so, doesn't it?" returned Dick, also in admiration. "I reckon the Dartaway will give a good account of herself, when she is properly handled. Now, I had better stop the propellers, I guess," he added, moving toward the front of the biplane to do so.

"Yes! yes! stop em!" yelled Tom, suddenly. "Hurry up, Dick! See how she is straining to break the ropes! Say, she wants to go up!"

Dick was startled and with good reason. Even while his brother was speaking there came a sudden snap, and one of the ropes flew apart. Then up out of the ground came the stake holding another rope. The big biplane, thus released on one side, slewed around, and Tom was knocked flat. Then came another snap and two more ropes flew apart.

"She's going! stop her!" screamed Tom, from where he lay, and the next moment he saw Dick struck full in the face by the machine. Down went the youth backwards, and as he fell, with a rush and a roar, the biplane sped over the level ground for a distance of two hundred feet and then went sailing into the air, headed almost point blank for the Rover homestead, less than fifty rods away!

CHAPTER II

SOMETHING ABOUT THE ROVER BOYS

"Oh, Dick, are you hurt?"

The cry came from Tom, as he turned over on the ground and struggled to his feet. He had seen his brother hurled backwards, and he saw that Dick made no move to arise. He had been struck in the head, and blood was flowing from a wound over his left ear.

"Oh, maybe he's killed!" gasped poor Tom, and then, for the moment he forgot all about the flying machine, that was rushing so madly through the air towards the Rover homestead. He hurried to his brother's side, at the same time calling for others to come to his assistance.

To my old readers the lads already mentioned will need no introduction. For the benefit of others let me state that the Rover boys were three in number, Dick being the oldest, funloving Tom coming next, and sturdy Sam being the youngest. They were the sons of Anderson Rover, a widower, and when at home, as at present, lived with their father and their Uncle Randolph and Aunt Martha at a pleasant place known as Valley Brook farm, in New York state.

While their father was in Africa on a mission of importance, the three boys had been sent by their uncle to boarding school, as related in the first volume of this series, entitled, "The Rover Boys at School." The place was Putnam Hall Military Academy, and there the lads had made many friends and also a few enemies.

From school the boys had made a short trip on the ocean, and then another trip into the jungle after their father. Then had followed a trip out West, and another on the Great Lakes. Later the youths had camped out in the mountains during the winter, shooting quite some game. Then they had returned to school, to go into camp during the summer with the other cadets.

The boys by this time thought their adventures at an end, but more were soon to follow. There came a long trip on land and sea, and then a voyage down the Ohio River, and soon after this the Rovers found themselves on the plains, where they had some adventures far out of the ordinary. From the plains they went further south, and in southern watersthe same being the Gulf of Mexicothey solved the mystery of the deserted steam yacht.

"Now back to the farm for me!" Sam had said at this time, and all were glad to go back, and also to return to Putnam Hall, from which seat of learning they presently graduated with honors. Then Mr. Anderson Rover got word of a valuable treasure, and he and the boys, with a number of their friends, went to Treasure Isle in search of it. They were followed by some of their enemies and the latter did all in their power to cause trouble.

Although the boys had finished at Putnam Hall, their days of learning were not yet over, and soon they set off for Brill College, a highgrade seat of learning located in one of our middlewestern states. They had with them an old school chum named John Powell, usually called "Songbird," because of his habit of making up and reciting socalled poetry, and were presently joined by another old school companion named William Philander Tubbs, a dudish chap who thought more of his dress and the society of ladies than he did of his studies. Tom loved to play jokes on Tubbs, who was generally too dense to see where the fun came in.

From the college the boys had taken another trip, as related in the fifteenth volume of this series, called "The Rover Boys Down East." There was a mystery about that trip, of which the outside world knew little, but as that trip has something to do with the events which are to follow in this story, I will here give such details as seem necessary.

When the Rover Boys went to Putnam Hall they met three girls, Dora Stanhope and her two cousins, Nellie and Grace Laning. Dora's mother was a widow, living not far from the school, and it was not long before a warm friendship sprang up between Dick and Dora, a friendship that grew more and more intimate as the days went by. Dick thought the world of Dora, and the two were now practically engaged to be married. As for Tom and Sam, they had taken to the two Laning girls from the start, and though Tom was too full of fun to pay much attention to girls, yet whenever Nellie was mentioned, he would grow red in the face; and it was noticed that whenever Grace was present Sam was usually on hand to keep her company.

The treasure unearthed on Treasure Isle had belonged to the Stanhope estate, the bulk of it going to Mrs. Stanhope and Dora and the remainder to the Lanings, because Mrs. Laning was Mrs. Stanhope's sister. But the treasure had been claimed by a certain rascal named Sid Merrick and his nephew, Tad Sobber, and when Merrick lost his life during a hurricane at sea, Sobber continued to do all he could to get the money and jewels into his possession.

"It's mine!" he told Dick Rover one day. "It's mine, all mine, and some day I'm going to get it!"

"You keep on, Tad Sobber, and some day you'll land in prison," had been Dick's answer. "We found that treasure, and the courts have decided that it belongs to the Stanhope estate, and you had better keep your hands off."

But Tad Sobber was not satisfied, and soon he made a move that caused the worst kind of trouble. There was a learned but unscrupulous man named Josiah Crabtree who had once been a teacher at Putnam Hall, but who had been discharged and who had, later on, been sent to prison for his misdeeds. This Josiah Crabtree had once sought to marry Mrs. Stanhope, thinking thereby to get control of her money and the money she held in trust for Dora. The lady was weak and sickly, and the teacher had tried to hypnotize her into getting married, and had nearly succeeded, but the plot was nipped in the bud by the Rover boys.

Tad Sobber met Josiah Crabtree and the pair hatched out another plot, this time to abduct Mrs. Stanhope, getting the lady at the time to bring a good share of the treasure with her under the impression that it was to be invested by her friends. The lady was carried off to an island in Casco Bay, off the coast of Maine, and thither the Rover boys and some others followed them. There was a good deal of excitement; but in the end the lady was rescued and the treasure brought back. An effort was made to capture Tad Sobber and Josiah Crabtree, but the two evildoers managed to get away.

The homecoming of the boys with Mrs. Stanhope had been a time of great rejoicing. Dora had embraced Dick over and over again for what he had done for her mother, and Nellie and Grace had not been backward in complimenting Tom and Sam on their good work. There had been a general jubilee which had lasted several days.

"Splendid work, boys, splendid work!" Anderson Rover had said. "I am proud of you!"

"Better work than the authorities could do," had come from Uncle Randolph.

"Now that treasure had better be placed where no outsider can get his hands on it," Mr. Rover had added. And soon after that it was put in the strong box of a safe deposit company, there to remain until it could be properly invested.

At Brill College the Rover boys had fallen in with a number of fine fellows, including Stanley Browne and a GermanAmerican student named Max Spangler. They had also encountered some others, among whom were Dudd Flockley, Jerry Koswell and Bart Larkspur. Led by Koswell, who was a thoroughly bad egg, the three lastnamed students had tried to get the Rover boys into trouble, and had succeeded. But they overreached themselves and were exposed, and in sheer fright Koswell and Larkspur ran away and refused to return. Dudd Flockley was repentant and was given another chance.

While on the hunt for Mrs. Stanhope, the Rovers had fallen in with Koswell and Larkspur. But instead of getting aid from the pair, the latter did what they could to help old Crabtree and Sobber. This brought on a fight, and Koswell and Larkspur received a thrashing they would long remember. The former college students might have been arrested, but, like Crabtree and Sobber, they kept out of sight.

"They are sure a bunch of bad ones," had been Dick Rover's comment, when referring to Crabtree, Sobber, Koswell and Larkspur. "I wish they were all in jail."

"I reckon we all wish that," had been Sam Rover's reply. "It's an awful shame that we didn't capture at least one of 'em."

"Well, we might have caught old Crabtree and Sobber if we hadn't broken the engine of the motorboat," put in Tom.

"Well, the engine was broken in a good cause," came from Dick. And he spoke the truth, as my old readers well know.

Following the homecoming of the boys, and the general jubilee, our heroes had settled down to enjoy themselves before going back to Brill. They had intended to take it easy on the farm, but when a great aviation meet was advertised to take place at the county seat they could not resist the temptation to be present.

At this meet there were five flying machines,three biplanes, a monoplane, and a dirigible balloon. All made good records, and the Rover boys became wildly enthusiastic over what they saw.

"Say, this suits me right down to the ground!" cried Tom.

"What fun a fellow could have if he had a flying machine and knew how to run it!" had come from Sam.

"Exactlyif he knew how to run it," had been Dick's words. "But if he didn't knowwell, he might have a nasty tumble, that's all."

"Pooh, Dick! If those fellows can run these machines, so can we," had been Tom's confident words.

"We know all about autos and motorboats," Sam had put in.

"That's true, Sam. But a monoplane or a biplane, or any kind of an aeroplane, isn't an auto or a motorboat."

"Are you afraid?" demanded Tom.

"Oh, no! Only if we got a flying machine we'd have to be careful about what we tried to do."

"Hurrah! It's settled!" cried Tom, who went headlong into everything. "We'll get a machine tomorrow! How much do they cost?"

"I don't knowseveral thousand dollars, I fancy," answered his elder brother.

"Boiled umbrellas, Dick! As much as that?"

"I think so."

"Why look at some of 'em," declared Sam. "Nothing but bamboo poles and a few wires, and canvas,and the engine!"

"Yes, but the poles, wires and canvas have to be put together just right, Sam, and those engines are as powerful as they are light. And then don't forget the propellers, and the steering outfit, and the other things."

"Come on and ask one of the men about them," came from Tom; and a little later they had a long talk with an aviator named Captain Colby, who proved to be a relative to Larry Colby, one of their former chums at Putnam Hall. He had heard about the Rover boys and some of their doings, and willingly told them all they wanted to know.

The boys went home with their minds full of flying machines, and as the Rovers were all welltodo, and as the three lads had in the past proved capable of taking care of themselves, it was not a very difficult matter for them to persuade their father to let them buy a biplane. Then, through Captain Colby, they learned where the flying machine could be obtained, and the very next day bought the affair and had it shipped to the farm, and also arranged with the aviator to visit them and give them a number of lessons.

"We've got three weeks before we have to go back to college," Tom had said. "If we are quick to learn we can have lots of fun in that time."

"Yes, and if we do learn, perhaps we can take the biplane to college with us and astonish some of the students and the faculty," Dick had added.

"That's the talk!" cried the youngest Rover. "We'll take it along!"

That morning Sam had gone off on an errand as already mentioned. Then Dick and Tom had gotten out the flying machine and started up the engine and the propellers. The ropes holding the biplane had broken or torn loose from the ground, and now the machine had gone off with a wild swoop, hurling poor Dick flat on his back and injuring him, how seriously was still to be learned.

CHAPTER III

SAM BRINGS NEWS

As Tom ran over to his brother's side he could not help but give a glance at the flying machine, which was rising higher and higher in the air, with a noise from the engine that sounded like a battery of gattling guns in action.

"Hi! hi! Wot's that?" came in a startled voice from the other side of the barn, and Jack Ness, the Rovers hired man, came running into view. "By gum, if them boys ain't gone an' flew without waitin' fer that man to show 'em! Who's doin' it? I don't see nobuddy." And the hired man blinked in amazement at the sight before him. "Is Sam in there?"

"Nobody is in the machine," answered Tom, who was kneeling beside his brother. "Oh, gracious! Look at that!" he exclaimed.

"There goes the chimbley!" roared Jack Ness, as the biplane swooped just high enough to clear the roof of the Rover homestead. One of the wheels underneath struck a chimney a glancing blow, hurling the bricks in all directions. As they came clattering down, from the house out ran Mrs. Rover, followed by her husband and the hired help. Anderson Rover was away on business.

"What is the matteris it aera cyclone?" gasped Randolph Rover.

"I don't know, I'm sure," answered Mrs. Rover. "But it's a terrible noise."

"Look! look!" shrieked the cook, pointing upward. "Saints preserve us!" she moaned. "'Tis the end of the world!"

"A flying machine!" murmured Randolph Rover. He gazed around hurriedly. "Can it be the boys?"

"Oh, those boys! They will surely kill themselves!" groaned Mrs. Rover. "They know nothing about airships!"

"Say, dar ain't nobuddy in dat contraption!" came suddenly from Aleck Pop. "It am flyin' all by itself!"

"By itself?" repeated Randolph Rover. "Impossible, Alexander! A flying machine cannot run itself. There must be somebody to steer, and manipulate the engine, and"

"Oh, maybe whoever was in it fell out!" screamed Mrs. Rover, and now she looked ready to faint.

"We must find out about this!" returned her husband quickly. "They had the machine in the shed back of the barn." And he ran in that direction, followed by the colored man, and then by his wife and the cook. In the meantime the biplane soared on and on, ever rising in the air and moving off in the direction of the river.

When the others arrived they found that Tom had carried poor Dick to the wagon shed and placed him on a pile of horse blankets, and was washing his wounded head with water. At the sight of her nephew lying there so still Mrs. Rover gave a scream.

"Oh, Tom, is heis he" she could not go on.

"He's only stunned, I guess, Aunt Martha," was the reply. "But he got a pretty good crack."

"Did the flying machine do it?" queried Randolph Rover.

"Yes. We had it tied fast, but when we started the engine and the propellers it broke loose and ran right over Dick."

"I dun tole you boys to be careful," burst out Aleck. "It's a suah wondah yo' ain't bof killed. Wot kin I do, Massa Tom?" And he got down on his knees beside Dick, for he loved these lads, who had done so much for him in the past.

"He's only stunned, I thinkand he's coming around now," answered Tom, and at that moment Dick commenced to stir. Then he gave a gasp, opened his eyes, and suddenly sat up.

"Stop her! Stop her, Tom!" he murmured.

"Dick! Dick, my poor, dear boy!" burst out Mrs. Rover, and got down beside him. "Oh, I am so thankful that you weren't killed!"

"Whyerwhy!" stammered the oldest Rover boy. "Say, what's happened?" he went on, looking from one to another of the group. "Where's the biplane?"

"Flew away," answered Tom. "You got struck and knocked down, don't you remember?"

"Ah!" Dick drew a deep breath. "Yes, I remember now. Oh, how my head aches!" He put up his hand and noticed the blood. "Got a pretty good rap, didn't I? What did the machine do, Tom; go to smash?"

"I don't know. The last I saw of her she was sailing over the house."

"She kept right on asailin'," answered Aleck. "Went on right ober de woods along de ribber."

"You don't say! Then we'll have a time of it getting her back." Dick gritted his teeth. "Phew! how my head hurts!"

"Bring him to the house, and we'll bind his head up," said Mrs. Rover. "I'll wash the wound first and we can put on some witch hazel."

"Yes, that or some peroxide of hydrogen," added Randolph Rover, who was a scientific farmer and something of a chemist. "That will kill any germs that may lodge there."

Dick was half led and half carried to the house and placed on a couch in the sitting room, and then his aunt went to work to make him comfortable. The cut was not a deep one, and the youth was suffering more from shock than from anything else.

"I'll be all right by tomorrow," he assured his Aunt Martha. "I only got a knockdown blow, that's all."

"The machine didn't fight fairly," added Tom, who had to have his little joke. "It hit Dick before he was ready."

"Well, I am thankful it was no worse," answered Mrs. Rover. "But it is bad enough."

"And we'll have to have a mason here to mend the chimney," added Randolph Rover.

"I'll get a man from the Corners tomorrow," said Tom. "But say, I'd like to know where the biplane went to," he continued anxiously.

"Maybe it landed on some other house," mused Randolph. "If it did you may have more to pay for than a dismantled chimney."

"Oh, houses are few and far between in that direction, Uncle Randolph. What I am afraid of is, that the biplane came down in the trees or on the rocks and got smashed. That would be a big loss."

"That is true."

"I can send Jack Ness and Aleck Pop out to look for the machine," went on Tom. "And I can go out myself with Sam, when he returns."

"Yes, you'd better do that," answered Dick. "And I'll go out with you tomorrow, if you can't locate the machine today."

"Better take it easy, Dick," cautioned his aunt.

"Oh, I'll be all right by tomorrow, Aunt Martha. A good night's sleep will be sure to set me on my feet again. And I can fix this cut up with a bit of adhesive plaster."

"Did you have much gasoline on board?" queried Randolph Rover.

"The tank was full," answered Tom. "Oh, the Dartaway could go a good many miles, if she wanted to," he added, dubiously.

"The Dartaway? Was that the name of the craft?"

"Yes, and she did dart away, didn't she?" and Tom grinned.

"For all we know, she may have gone fifty or a hundred miles," continued Dick. "But I doubt it. With nobody to steer she'd be bound to turn turtle or something before long."

"Well, if she's busted, she's busted, that's all," answered Tom, philosophically. Yet the thought of the beautiful biplane being a wreck caused him to sigh.

A few minutes later the honk of an automobile horn was heard in the lane leading to the house, and Sam Rover appeared, driving the family car. He was alone on the front seat and in the tonneau had a variety of things purchased in the village for his aunt and the others.

"Hello! what does this mean?" cried Sam, as he came into the sitting room and saw Dick with his head bound up. "What did you do? Did you get that fussing with the biplane?"

"I did, Sam," was the answer.

"We both had a setto with her ladyship," put in Tom. "And the biplane floored us on the first round." And then he told his younger brother of what had occurred.

"Humph! that's too bad!" murmured Sam. He took Dick's hand. "Not hurt much, really?" he asked in a lower voice.

"No, Sam, I'll soon be O. K."

"Jumping lobsters! But this beats all!" went on the youngest Rover. "I don't know if I had better tell you or not." And he looked around, to see if anybody but his brothers was present. The grown folks had left the room.

"Tell us what?" demanded Tom, who quickly saw that Sam had something on his mind.

"Tell you the news."

"What news?" asked Dick.

"Maybe you can't stand it, Dick. It will keep till tomorrow."

"See here, Sam, I'm not a baby," retorted the oldest Rover boy. "If you've got anything worth telling tell it."

"But it may make your head ache worse, Dick."

"No, it won't. Now, what's the news? Out with it."

Instead of answering at once, Sam Rover walked over to the door and closed it carefully.

"No use of worrying the others about it," he half whispered.

"But what is it?" demanded Tom, and now he showed that he was as impatient as was Dick.

"I got a letter from Grace Laning," went on Sam, slowly, and turned a bit red. "She told me a piece of news that is bound to upset you, Dick."

"Is it about the Stanhopesabout Dora?" questioned Dick, half rising from the couch on which he rested.

"Yes,and about some others, too. But don't get excited. Nothing very bad has happened, yet."

"What did happen, Sam? Hurry up and tell us,don't keep us in suspense!" cried Dick.

"Well; then, if you want it in a few words, here goes. Grace was visiting the Stanhopes a few days ago and she and Dora went to Ithaca to do some shopping. While in that town, coming along the street leading to the boat landing, they almost ran into Tad Sobber and old Josiah Crabtree."

"What! Those rascals in that townso near to the Stanhope home!" exclaimed Dick. "And after what has happened! We must have them arrested!"

"I don't think you can do it, Dicknot from what Grace says in her letter."

"What does she say?"

"She says she and Dora were very much frightened, especially when they discovered that both Sobber and old Crabtree had been drinking freely. The two got right in front of the girls and commenced to threaten them and threaten us. Nobody else was near, and the girls didn't know what to do. But at last they got away and ran for the boat, and what became of Sobber and old Crabtree they don't know."

"What did the rascals say to them?" questioned Tom, who could see that his brother had not told all of his tale.

"They said that they were going to square up with Dora and with Mrs. Stanhope, and said they would square up with us, too, and in a way we little expected. Grace wrote that Sobber pulled a big roll of bank bills out of his pocket and flourished it in her face. 'Do you see that?' he asked. 'Well, I can get more where that came from, and I am going to use that and more, too, just to get even with the Rovers. I'm getting my trap set for them, and when they fall into it they'll wish they had never been born! I'll blow them and their whole family skyhigh, that's what I'll do.'"

"Sobber said that?" asked Dick, slowly.

"So Grace writes. No wonder she and Dora were scared to death."

"Oh, maybe he was only blowing, especially if he had been drinking too much," came from Tom.

"I don't know about that," answered Dick, with a long sigh. "With such a rascal at liberty,and with money in his pocketthere is no telling what will happen."

"What do you suppose he meant by blowing us skyhigh?" asked Tom. But this question was not answered, for at that moment Mrs. Rover came into the room, and the course of the conversation had to be changed,the lads not wishing to worry her with their new troubles.

CHAPTER IV

AT THE TELEPHONE

Tom and Sam spent the balance of the day in looking for the missing biplane, walking down to the river, and even visiting Humpback Falls, where the youngest Rover had once had such a thrilling adventure.

"Don't seem to be in sight," remarked Tom, after they had tramped through the woods and over the rocks until they were tired.

"Looks to me as if the Dartaway had gone further than we supposed possible," replied Sam. "Maybe she's a hundred miles from here."

"Oh, she may have gone clean over to the ocean and dropped in," said Tom. "But I don't see how she couldwith nobody to steer. How long would an auto keep to the road without somebody steering?"

"Do you know what I think we ought to do? Go back home and telephone to the villages and towns in the direction the biplane took. Somebody must have seen the craft,if she kept in the air."

"By Jove, Sam, that's the idea! Why didn't you think of that before? It would have saved us quite a tramp."

The two boys turned back, and reached home a little after the supper hour. The meal had been held back for them.

"Any luck?" asked Dick, who sat in an easy chair on the front piazza. His cuts had been plastered up and he felt quite like himself again.

"No luck; but Sam has an idea," answered Tom, and mentioned what it was.

"You must have supper first," said Mrs. Rover. "Then you can do all the telephoning you please." And so it was agreed.

During the past few months the telephone service in the neighborhood of Dexter's Corners had been greatly improved and the lines could be connected with nearly all of the villages and towns roundabout.

21

"I'll try Carwood first," said Sam. "I'll call up Tom Bender. He's a wideawake fellow and would know if an airship had been seen."

Carwood was soon had on the wire and Sam presently was talking to the boy he had mentioneda lad who worked in the general store with his father.

"See an airship?" cried Tom Bender. "We sure didscooting over this burgh like a streak, too! Was it your machine? Who was running it? I tried to make out but couldn't."

"Nobody was running it," answered Sam. "It ran away on its own account, from back of our barn. Where did it go to?"

"Ran away! Suffering toadstools, Sam, you don't mean it! I don't know where it went, it went so fast."

"Which way was it headed? Try to tell me as nearly as you can."

"It was headed over Bear Hill, near the Spring. That would about take it over Rayville."

"Thank you, Tom; then I'll call up somebody in Rayville. Goodbye."

"Oh, say, Sam, hold on a minute. You say the machine broke away. How was that?" Tom Bender was all curiosity.

"We were trying the engine and propellers, that's all. I'll tell you the rest when I see you," answered the youngest Rover, and rang off. "Tom would keep me answering questions for a year if I let him," he added, to his brothers.

He next tried the Rayville general store, but could get no information concerning the missing biplane. Then he tried several farmers who were utter strangers to him but whose names were in the telephone directory.

"Airship, eh?" queried one farmer, a man named Peter Marley. "Well, we sure did see an airship, fer it came nigh onto rippin' off the roof o' the barn. Ef I had the feller here as was runin' it I'd give him a dose o' buckshot! He nigh scart my wife into a fit, he did!"

"Which way did the airship go, Mr. Marley?"

"Went right over into Rocker's Woods,over where the old saw mill used to be."

"Did the airship come down, do you think?"

"I guess soleas'wise she looks like she was goin' to come down. But who was the crazy loon as was runnin' her?"

"Nobody was running the craftshe ran away on her own hook."

"By gum! Ye don't tell me! No wonder she acted so blamed crazy like! Any reward fer her?" And the farmer's voice betrayed a sudden interest.

"I don't knowI'll find out," answered Sam, and then consulted hastily with his brothers.

"Tell him the biplane is ours and if he will help locate it and get it to a safe place we will pay him well for his services," said Dick.

"When can we go to Rayville?"

"First thing in the morning. There's a good road, and we can make the sixteen miles in the auto in no time."

"All right," said Sam, and told Peter Marley of what had been said. The farmer agreed to remain around his house until they arrived and then do all in his power to help locate the Dartaway.

"Dick, do you think you'll be able to take that trip?" questioned Randolph Rover. "Hadn't you better remain behind? I can go with Tom and Sam if necessary."

"Oh, I'll be all right in the morning," was the reply.

"But you've got to let me and Sam run the machine," put in Tom. "No use of your doing that."

"All right," answered the eldest Rover boy.

That night, when the others had gone to bed, the three Rover boys gathered in Dick's room to discuss further the news regarding Josiah Crabtree and Tad Sobber.

"Do you suppose it is possible that Sobber thinks to come here and blow the house up?" queried Tom.

"He might be equal to it," answered Dick, soberly. "We'll have to keep our eyes peeled, and, when we go back to Brill, we'll have to warn dad and Uncle Randolph."

"Do you know, dad looked worried when he went away," put in Sam.

"I noticed it, Sam. Did he say anything to you about business?"

"Not a word. Why, do you think it's that?"

"There is some trouble out westhas been ever since there was a strike at that Golden Horseshoe mine in which dad invested so heavily last summer. They had a strike, and now one crowd is trying to get the control from another crowd. I don't know the particulars, but I guess dad is worried."

"Dick, don't you think you ought to help him in these affairs?" came suddenly from Sam. "Uncle Randolph is too absorbed in his books and in scientific farming to pay any attention, andwell, dad isn't as young as he used to beand we are growing older."

"I've been thinking of that, Sam. I wish I was through college, I'd jump right into the game and try to take the load from his shoulders."

"Are you going to take the full course?"

"No, I talked it over with dad last week and I'm going to take the shorter course. He said you two could take the long course if you wanted to."

"Not much! The short course for yours truly!" cried Tom.

"Ditto here!" came from Sam.

"I want to settle down and get into business," went on Tom.

"He thinks Nellie won't wait much longer," remarked Sam, with a wink at Dick.

"Huh! I guess, you think Grace won't wait!" snorted Tom. "Didn't I see you looking over that furniture and picture catalogue the other day? Ha! I caught you, Sammy, my boy!"

"Rats!" cried Sam, growing suddenly red in the face. "I was thinking of buying a new chair and maybe a picture or two for our quarters at Brill. The old ones are pretty punk, if you'll remember. Besides, we've got to wait until Dick and Dora step off, you know," went on the youngest Rover.

"That's soso we have," added Tom, with more of a grin than ever. "By the way, Dick, how much longer are you going to linger before you scrape up money enough to pay the minister's fee?"

"Just long enough to hammer some commonsense into the heads of two brothers of mine!" cried Dick, and threw a book at Tom and a pillow at Sam. "Now go to bed and don't forget to wake up early, for we want to be in Rayville by eight o'clock, so we can have all day, if necessary, to locate the biplane." And then he chased Tom and Sam out of the bedroom and locked the door on them.

Left to himself, Dick walked slowly across the room to where the bureau stood. On the top was a small, framed picture of Dora Stanhope, that had been taken only a few months before. Dick could not help but take up the portrait and gaze at it long and earnestly.

"Dear, dear Dora!" he murmured fondly. "The best girl in all this wide world! Some day you are going to be Mrs. Dick Rover, and that day can't come any too soon for me. Oh, I hope those rascals don't do anything more to harm you!"

Dick was still holding the picture when there came a soft knock on the door.

"Who is it? What do you want?" he asked, as he put the picture down.

"Dick, my child," came in a whisper from the funloving Tom. "Be careful and don't kiss all the glaze off that photo. She's a sweet girl, warranted all silk and a yard wide, but the glaze may be poisonous, and"

"Tom, if you don't get to bed I'llI'll throw a pitcher of water over you!" cried Dick, and started to unlock the door. With a merry laugh Tom ran off; and that was the last seen or heard of him that night.

Before retiring Dick gave his wounded head another application of liniment, and in the morning he was gratified to find that much of the soreness was gone. The cuts, of course, remained, and he bound these up with extra strips of adhesive plaster. The three lads had an early breakfast, and by halfpast seven o'clock were in the touring car, bound for Rayville.

"How are you going to get the biplane back here, even if you do find it?" questioned their uncle, before they started off.

"I don't know," answered Dick. "It will depend on what condition the Dartaway is in. She may be so broken up as to be unfit for anything, and then it wouldn't pay to move her."

"Well, better not attempt to fly in the craft," cautioned Randolph Rover.

"Hardly," said Tom. "Maybe we'll telephone for Captain Colby to come and get her."

Tom was at the wheel of the touring car and, once the farm was left behind, and they were on a fairly good country road, he advanced the spark and the gasoline control until they were running at twentyfive and then thirty miles an hour.

"Now, don't get gay, Tom!" warned Dick. "This road wasn't built for racing."

"Pooh, what's thirty miles an hour!" declared the funloving Rover, who just then felt like "letting out." "You know this machine can make fifty and better, Dick."

"I know it, but you've got to have a safer road than this, Tom."

"Beware of the turn!" cried Sam, who sat on the front seat with Tom, while Dick was alone in the tonneau. "It's a bad one!"

"I know it, but I'll make it," answered Tom, and then the touring car reached a bend in the road, and went whizzing around it with a sudden lurch that made Sam cling desperately to the seat and sent Dick flying from one side of the tonneau to the other.

"Tom, be careful!" cried Sam. "Do you want to pitch me out on my head?"

"Do that again, and I'll make you let Sam drive," came from Dick.

"It was the brakeit didn't act just right," answered Tom, just a little frightened. "I think it's loose."

"Better stop and look at it," answered Dick, promptly.

"Oh, I guess it's all right," said Tom. The touring car continued to move along, up a winding hill. Then came a level stretch for half a mile, and then a sharp descent, leading into Carwood.

"Now be careful" commenced Dick. And then stopped short, for a sudden snapping sound reached his ears.

26

"What's that?" cried Sam, in alarm.

"The brakeit's broken!" answered Tom. And then he set his teeth grimly, to try to guide the heavy touring car down the steep hill without disaster.

CHAPTER V

LOOKING FOR THE LOST FLYING MACHINE

It was the foot brake that had given away. The hand brake was still fit for use, but each of the Rover boys remembered with dismay that this brake had been loose for some time. They had thought to tighten it up, but other matters had claimed their attention, and they had not deemed it absolutely necessary before taking the short trip to Rayville, since on starting the other brake had seemed to be in good order.

"Can you do it, Tom?" asked Dick, quickly, as the big car gathered headway on the steep hill.

"I'll try!" was Tom's reply. "But it's some hill."

"If only we don't meet anything," put in Sam. "Blow the horn, Dick!"

The oldest Rover boy did as requested, leaning over from the back seat to do so, and thus leaving Tom free to manipulate the steering wheel. Dick also set the hand brake a notch tighter, but this did little good, since it was the bands that were worn.

On and on bounded the touring car, down the long hill. On both sides the road was bound by rocks and trees, with nasty gullies in several spots. Here and there were "resting spots" for teams, and over these indentations flew the automobile with jolts that threatened to break all the springs at once.

"The turn! Beware of the turn!" cried Sam and Dick together, when about threequarters of the hill had been passed.

Tom nodded but said not a word. He had thrown the motive power to the low gear, and thus the engine was doing something towards holding the car back.

Suddenly Dick uttered a cry, and the next minute Sam saw him dive down to the bottom of the tonneau and bring up several long ropes to which were attached a number of hooks. He had placed these in the automobile for possible use in getting the Dartaway out of the woods or from among the rocks.

28

With care Dick took the hooks and threw them out of the machine. At the same time he leaned over and allowed the ends of the ropes to catch on the swiftlyrevolving wheels of the machine.

"Maybe they'll hold somethinganyway I hope so," he said.

They had now reached the turn. Tom was running as closely as possible to the inner side and Dick had commenced to toot the horn again. With a slipping and sliding, the touring car went over the dirt and stones, rushing nearer and nearer to the gully on the outer edge of the highway.

"Look! Look!" screamed Sam, a second later. "A carriage, and three ladies in it!"

He was right, and the carriage was less than a hundred yards ahead. But just now Tom could think of nothing but the turn, for the machine was running closer than ever to the gully. If they went down in that the touring car would most likely turn turtle, and they might all be killed.

But they did not go down into the gully. By sheer good luck Tom managed to throw the automobile back into the roadway, two wheels for a second spinning in midair. Then he had to reckon with the other dangerthat of hitting the carriage with the three ladies.

The ladies had heard the tooting of the auto horn and had tried to draw up to the side of the road. But the incline was still steep and the two horses evidently did not like the looks of that gully.

"You can't pass them!" groaned Sam, and just then came a grinding from underneath the touring car. This was followed by a series of jerks, and then came one final jerk that brought the automobile to a standstill and all but sent the Rover boys flying over the engine hood.

"Well, we've stopped!" panted Tom, when he could catch his breath. "I guess the brake held somehow."

"No, it didn't," answered Sam. "It's another brake, one that Dick heaved overboard." And he pointed to the ropes and hooks. One hook, the biggest, had caught in a rock lining the gully, and the ropes were in a mess around the wheels and the rear axle.

"Good for you!" murmured Tom. "It saved us from running into that carriage."

"Are you men going on?" cried one of the ladies, noticing that the automobile had come to a stop.

"Not just yet!" sang out Dick. "You can go ahead if you wish. We'll wait until you get down to the bottom of the hilland maybe we'll wait longer," he added in an undertone.

"You scared us nearly to death," said another of the ladies, tartly; and then the carriage went on and was soon lost to sight on a side road.

The three youths alighted, and after blocking the wheels with stones, so that it might not get away unexpectedly, commenced an inspection of the car.

"The ropes wouldn't do much damage but the hooks might," said Dick. "But I couldn't think of anything else to do."

"It was grand of you to do that," answered Tom, warmly. "I was a fool to let her out as I did," he added bluntly. "I'll know better next time."

That was Tom, often headstrong but quick to acknowledge a fault.

Not without much difficulty did the three youths manage to get the ropes disentangled from the rear wheels and the back axle. It was found that one of the hooks had gone into a tire, causing a blowout that, in the general excitement, nobody had noticed. But otherwise everything seemed to be all right, apart, of course, from the broken brake rod, and the boys were thankful.

"I guess we can manage to run to the nearest blacksmith shop," said Dick, "and there we can get the rod mended."

"What a lucky thing that big hook caught in the rock!" cried Sam.

"It's the one thing that saved us from going into the carriage," returned Tom, and his face was very sober as he spoke. For a time being he did not feel like running the car further and readily agreed to let Sam take hold, after another tire had been adjusted. To keep the automobile from going down the remainder of the hill too rapidly, they allowed one of the ropes to remain on the rear axle, and to this tied a small fallen tree, that made an excellent drag.

When the level roadway was gained once more they made good time to Carwood, and there called on the blacksmith to repair the broken brake rod. While waiting they ran into Tom Bender, and the boy was very anxious to know all about the lost aeroplane.

"Say, but you fellows have a cinch!" he said, in admiration. "You get what you please. Wish I was in your shoes!"

"You'd not want to be in our shoes when that brake rod broke," answered Sam bluntly. "Eh, Tom?"

"Not much!" replied his brother.

At last they were on the way again. They had telephoned to Peter Marley, so that the farmer would know the cause of the delay. Sam did the driving and now the machine went along well, and almost before they knew it they were at Rayville and asking the way to the Marley farm. This was on a back road, but the way was good and they reached the farm without trouble, excepting that they had to slow down to let a herd of cows pass them.

"Got here at last, have ye!" cried Peter Marley, as he came out to greet them. "You kin put that 'mobile under the wagon shed if ye want to," he added.

"Can't we use it to go after the biplane?" questioned Dick.

"No, there hain't no fit road. If ye say so, we can go on hossesif ye want to pay fer ridin'," added the farmer shrewdly. He was a good man, but close, and never allowed a chance to make an honest cent slip by.

"All right, we'll ride," said Dick. "The horses may come in handy for hauling the biplane,and besides, we can't carry these ropes and hooks if we walk."

So it was arranged; and a little later the party of four set off on horseback, the farmer and Tom carrying the ropes and hooks, and Sam keeping beside Dick, who looked a trifle pale in spite of his efforts to appear all right. The knockdown blow from the flying machine had been harder than the eldest Rover boy was willing to admit.

Rocker's Woods proved to be a large patch of scrub timber, all the large trees having been cut down to feed the old sawmill, which still stood on the bank of a goodsized stream. The sawmill had not been used for nine years and the timber was gradually coming up once more.

"This is exactly the way thet airship tuk," said Peter Marley, as he led the way. "An' as she wasn't runnin' very fast I guess she must acome down not very fur off."

"I hope so," answered Dick. "And I hope, too, she came down gently."

"Huh! How could she come down any other way? Ain't much to 'em, is there, 'ceptin' sticks an' cloth."

"The engine weighs several hundred pounds."

"Gee shoo! Several hundred pounds! Say, if thet's so, it's great how they kin stay up!" burst out the farmer in admiration. "Ain't no bird as weighs as much as thet!"

As they advanced through the woods, all of the party looked to the right and the left for some sign of the missing biplane.

"Here's a tree top down!" cried Tom, when they were close to the river on which the old saw mill was located. "This looks as if it might have been done by the machine."

"Gracious, I wonder if the airship went into the river!" burst out Sam.

"That might be a good thing, if it did," answered Dick. "It might save it from being wrecked, and we might be able to tow it ashore."

In a moment more they came to a halt at the edge of the river, which was broad and smooth at this point. In the middle the stream was ten to twelve feet deep, and the bottom was of sand and smooth rocks.

"I don't see anything that looks like a flying machine," said Sam after a long look around.

"Maybe after all it went over into the woods on the other side," returned Dick.

"That must be it," said Peter Marley. "I'm afraid we'll have to go up the stream a bit to get across. We can't ford here."

"How far to a good ford?" asked Dick.

"About quarter o' a mile tudder side o' the old mill."

"Say, look over there!" cried Tom at this moment. "What does that look like to you, Sam?"

He pointed with his hand, and all in the party gazed in the direction indicated, a point close to the opposite shore, where some brushwood overhung the river.

"Why that looks to me like one of the planes of the flying machine!" cried the youngest Rover.

"Just what I thought," exclaimed Tom. "What do you say, Dick?"

"It certainly does look like one of the planes," answered the older brother. "But don't be too sure, or we may be disappointed."

"Too bad we can't get over here," murmured Sam. "Supposing I swim it?" he continued.

"No, don't bother, Sam," replied Dick. "We'll all go around by way of the ford. You can't do anything alone anyway."

"But I might make sure if it was the machine," insisted Sam.

"Never mind; we want to get over there anywayto continue the searchif that isn't the machine."

Again Peter Marley led the way, along a trail that ran past the old mill. The boys came close at his heels, and as they advanced Tom questioned the farmer concerning the place.

"It belongs to a lumber company, but it's been closed up fer years," said Peter Marley. "Once in a while tramps hang out there, but thet's all."

Presently they found themselves close to the mill, which was almost ready to fall down from disuse and neglect. As they rode up Tom chanced to glance towards a side window and was surprised to catch sight of a man looking curiously at them. As soon as he saw that he was discovered the man stepped out of sight.

"Well, I never!" gasped Tom. "Did you see him?"

"See who?" asked his brothers.

"That man at the window of the mill! Unless I am greatly mistaken it was Josiah Crabtree!"

CHAPTER VI

TWO OLD ENEMIES

"Josiah Crabtree!" came simultaneously from Dick and Sam Rover.

"Yes," returned Tom.

"How can he be here, in this outoftheway place?" demanded Sam.

"You must be mistaken, Tom," came from the eldest Rover boy. "Old Crabtree must be around Cedarville or in Ithaca. He would have no call to come to a place like this."

"Did you say Josiah Crabtree?" questioned Peter Marley, curiously. All had come to a halt on their horses.

"Yes," returned Tom quickly. "Do you know him?"

"I used to know himfact is, he once stopped at my place to git a ridewhen he was avisitin' thet old mill."

"Then he visits the mill!" exclaimed Dick. "Tom, you must have been right."

"But why does he come here?" questioned Sam.

"Why as near as I know, some relative o' his'n used to have an interest in the lumber company as run the mill," replied the farmer. "It was a man named Foxwell. He's dead now. Maybe he left his share o' the place to this man Crabtree. He was a teacher, wasn't he?"

"He was, years ago. Since then he has been a jailbird," answered Tom.

"A jailbird!"

"Yes, he was in jail for a number of yearsand since he has been out he has been trying his best to make trouble for us and for some of our friends," went on Tom. "Come on, let's go after him, instead of talking," he added, as he dismounted.

"That's the talk!" cried Sam. "The biplane can wait."

34

Dick was as willing as his brothers to go after the former teacher of Putnam Hall, and leaving the farmer to take care of the horses, all three ran up to the door of the old mill. It was unlocked, and one of the hinges was broken, and it was an easy matter for them to push their way into the building.

"Do you think Tad Sobber is with old Crabtree?" asked Sam, in a low voice.

"It may besince they were together when the girls saw them," returned Dick.

"We ought to have armed ourselves," put in Tom. The boys had no weapons of any kind.

"Here are some old barrel staves," said Tom. "They are better than nothing." And he picked up a stave and his brothers followed suit.

With caution the three Rover boys advanced through the old mill, which, because of the closed doors and dirty windows, was a gloomy place in spite of the brightness of the day outside. All listened intently, but not a sound reached their ears, excepting Mr. Marley's voice as he talked to the restless horses.

"Supposing I call to him?" suggested Dick.

"It can't do any harm," answered Sam.

"Hello, Mr. Crabtree!" sang out Tom, without waiting for his brother. "Where are you? Why don't you show yourself?"

All waited after this call. But no reply came back, and then Dick and Sam called.

"He's a bit bashful," was Tom's grinning comment. "Wants to be hauled out by the coattails, I guess. Come on, we'll soon locate him," and he started forward.

"Be careful, Tom!" warned his elder brother. "He may set a trap for you! You know he and Sobber are not to be trusted."

"I've got my eyes open," answered the funloving Rover sturdily.

With the barrel staves in hand, the three Rover boys advanced further and further into the old mill, going from one room to another. Occasionally they stumbled over bits of lumber and piles of sawdust, for when the place had been shut down no attempt had been made to clean up. Even some of the machinery had been left and this was now so rusted that it was practically unfit for use.

"Say, Mr. Crabtree, why don't you show yourself?" called out Dick. "Are you afraid?"

"You get out of here!" came the unexpected answer, from a small toolroom, the door to which was split but tightly closed. "You Rovers have no right on this property!"

The boys recognized the harsh and dictatorial voice of Josiah Crabtree,less pleasant now than it ever had been. They saw the former teacher glaring at them from the split in the toolroom door.

"Mr. Crabtree, come out here and let us talk to you," said Dick, quietly but firmly.

"I don't want to talk to youI want you to leave these premises," snarled the man.

"Why should we leave?" asked Tom.

"Because this is my property."

"Your property?" cried Sam. "How so?"

"It was left to me by a distant relative. I won't have you on the place."

"Mr. Crabtree, do you know that we can have you arrested?" said Dick, sharply.

"Arrested? What for?"

"For the abduction of Mrs. Stanhope."

"I didn't abduct hershe went along of her own free willI can prove it."

"You know that statement is false. You carried her off against her willand did what you could to hypnotize her into marrying you. Mr. Crabtree, you are a villain, and you ought to be returned to the prison from which you came."

"Don't you dare to talk to me like that! Don't you dare!" fairly shrieked Josiah Crabtree. "I know my rights, and some day I'll have the law on you boys! You are responsible for my being sent to prison, and but for you Mrs. Stanhope would have married me long ago. Now I want you to leave these premises, and don't you dare to come back."

36

"Is Tad Sobber with you?" asked Tom.

"I am not here to answer questions, Tom Rover. I want to leave, and at once."

"Mr. Crabtree, you listen to me," said Dick, stepping closer to the crack in the door. "We are not afraid of you, and we want you and Tad Sobber to know it. Were it not for the unpleasant publicity for Mrs. Stanhope and her daughter, we'd have you in the lockup inside of twentyfour hours. We understand that you and Sobber have been threatening the Stanhopes and the Lanings again, and also threatening us. Now these threats have got to stop, and you have got to behave yourself. If you don't behave yourself we are going to make it our business to see that you are arrested, and we'll do our level best to have you placed behind the bars for a long term of years."

"Ilwiller" stammered the former teacher of Putnam Hall. He did not know how to proceed.

"Ah, don't you get scared!" came in a low voice from inside the toolroom. "You know what the Rovers are."

"It must be Tad Sobber!" cried Tom. "Sobber, if you are in there why don't you show yourself? Are you scared?"

"Of course he is scared," put in Sam.

"I'm not scared!" roared the bullying voice of the youth who had claimed the fortune from Treasure Isle. "I am not scared and you know it."

"So you are really there, Sobber," put in Dick. "I thought as much. Well, you heard what I said to Crabtree. It applies to you as well."

"Bah, Dick Rover, you can't scare me!" returned Tad Sobber savagely. "Just now you think you are on top. But wait, that's all. That treasure belongs to me and I mean to have it. And I mean to square up for the way you have treated me, too."

"Are you two going to settle down here?" asked Sam, just for something to say.

"That is none of your business," answered Josiah Crabtree. "Now I want you to leave."

"Sobber, what has become of Jerry Koswell and Bart Larkspur?" asked Dick, wishing to know something of those former goodfornothing students of Brill College.

"Never you mind what has become of them," answered Sobber. "But don't think you have seen the last of them, Dick Rover. They haven't forgotten how you treated them on Chesoque Island and elsewhere, and they mean to even up that score."

"Are they here with you?"

"No. But I'm going to keep in touch with them, and some day we But never mind now. Just you wait, that's all!" finished Tad Sobber, meaningly.

"You'll try to play us foul,just as you tried in the past," said Dick. "Very well, I'll remember that, Sobber. And you remember what I told you. The next time there is trouble we'll fight it out to the bitter end."

There was a moment of silence.

"I want you to go away," said Josiah Crabtree, and there was just a trace of nervousness in his tones. Evidently Dick's firm words had had some effect.

"We are going," answered Dick. "Both of you remember what I said." And then he motioned to his brothers; and all three left the old mill.

"Well, did ye find the feller ye was after?" queried Peter Marley, as the boys came out to where he stood with the horses.

"We did," answered Dick, and nudged his brothers, to keep them quiet. "It's Josiah Crabtree all right. And we had quite a talk with him."

"Wot's he going to do here?"

"He says it is his propertyleft to him by a distant relative. He ordered us away."

"Must have been Foxwell left him the place. Is he going to start the mill up ag'in?"

"He didn't say."

"If he's a jailbird I'll hate to see him in these parts," went on the farmer soberly.

"Well, it won't hurt you to keep an eye on him, Mr. Marley," answered Dick, and then, struck with a sudden idea, he continued: "And if you see or hear anything wrong about him, will you do us the favor to let us know at once, over the telephone, or otherwise? I'll pay you for the calls."

"Sure I'll let you knowif I hear anything."

"I might as well tell you that he is down on us and down on some of our friends, and he and a young fellow with him named Tad Sobber may try to play us foul in some way. So, if you hear of anything strange, let us know by all means."

"You can depend on it, I will," replied Peter Marley.

"And now to see if that really was the biplane!" cried Tom, when the party was once more on horseback. "Let us try to forget old Crabtree and Sobber. One trouble at a time is enough. If that was the flying machine, I hope she isn't damaged much," he added, wistfully, for he had hoped to get a good deal of sport out of sailing the Dartaway.

"Well, if that was the biplane, she must have landed in the river, and that would break the shock some," said Sam, hopefully.

"Yes, especially if she came down on a slant," added Dick. "Maybe she struck the water and scaled along like a clamshell."

Along the river they proceeded for quite a distance and then came to the spot that the farmer said was the ford.

"Not so very shallow either," was Dick's comment. "Mr. Marley, are you sure of the footing?"

"Yes, I've been across any number of times," was the answer. "I'll lead the way. Be careful, fer the rocks is slippery an' if a hoss goes down he might give ye a nasty tumble."

And then Peter Marley urged his steed into the river and one by one the Rover boys followed him.

CHAPTER VII

THE RUNAWAY HORSES

In the middle of the river the ford was so deep that the water almost touched the feet of the riders. But fortunately the current was sluggish, so the horses managed to keep their footing. They were allowed to take their own time, so it took several minutes to gain the opposite shore.

"Well, I'm glad we are out of that," was Tom's comment, as they reached a trail on the other bank.

"We'll have to endure it again, to get back," said Sam. "And what about the biplane?"

"Just wait till we find the machine first," answered Dick, with a faint smile. "You know the old saying, 'Don't count your chickens'"

"Before they are fried," finished Tom, with a grin. "You see, somebody might lift them from the henroost before you had a chance to cook them," he went on soberly.

"By gum! thet ain't no joke nuther!" burst in Peter Marley. "Many a chicken I've lost through tramps an' wuthless niggers."

"THERE SHE IS!" BURST FROM TOM'S LIPS.
They had to go around several walls of rocks and through a tangle of brushwood, and then came to a small clearing where was located the remains of a woodcutter's hut. Not far beyond was the locality where they had seen the object that looked like one of the biplane's wings.

It must be confessed that the hearts of the three boys beat a bit faster as they drew closer. Would they find the flying machine, and if so, would it be in serviceable condition or so smashed up as to be worthless?

"There she is!" burst from Tom's lips, and he pointed out into the water.

"Right down between half a dozen big rocks," added Sam. "Is she smashed much? How about the engine, Dick?"

"The engine is there, but I can't tell if it's broken or not. We'll soon find out."

40

The big biplane lay among some rocks and bushes, the latter overhanging the water, which at this spot was less than two feet deep. By taking off their shoes and socks, and rolling up their trousers, the boys were able to wade out to the flying machine and make an inspection.

"One of the planes is broken," said Dick. "But as the bamboo poles are merely split I think they can be repaired with some fine wire,just as we repair a split baseball bat."

"But the engine?" asked Sam, impatiently.

"I think the engine is all rightat least it looks all right to me. Of course we can't be sure until we clean it up and try it."

"Then she must have struck the water on the slant and that must have broken the shock," said Tom; and this surmise was undoubtedly correct, for had the Dartaway come down squarely on the rocks the planes and the engine must have been broken to bits.

"Do you think we can get her ashore?" asked Sam.

"Sure we can, by the aid of the hooks and ropes, and the horses. But we want to be careful how it's done. There is no sense in breaking the machine still more."

"We might get some planks from that old hut and roll the wheels up on them," suggested Tom. "I don't believe anybody uses the hut."

"No, that ain't been used for years," said Peter Marley. "Ye can tear down the hull thing if ye want to."

The boys and the farmer set to work, and presently they had several rough planks taken from the sides of the hut. They had the horses drag these down to the water, and by hard work managed to get the planks under the flying machine. As the planks were of wood they aided in floating the affair.

"By jinks! I've got an idea!" suddenly cried Dick. "We'll want the machine on the other side of the river. Why not build a raft and float her over instead of bringing her ashore here? There is plenty of stuff in that old hut."

"That's the ticket!" answered Tom. "Hurrah for a life on the rolling deep!"

"It's a good idee," was the farmer's comment. "I was wonderin' how we'd git over with the contraption. You kin keep on shovin' planks an' logs under till she floats, an' tie them together with the ropes ye brung along. A good idee."

It was not until noon that they had the socalled raft built and the biplane fastened to it. The work had made them all hungry and they were glad that they had brought along a substantial lunch. They sat down in the shade of the woods to eat, washing the meal down with some water from a spring back of the old hut,or rather of what was now left of the structure. While the boys ate they talked about Josiah Crabtree and Tad Sobber and the others who were their enemies.

"They'll surely try to do something," said Dick. "But what it will be I can't guess. We'll have to keep on guard."

"Who is going to go on the raft?" asked Sam. "It won't carry all of us."

"I'll pole it over," answered Dick. "The rest of you will have to go around by the ford."

"Don't you want any help?" asked Tom.

"No, I think I can do it alone. If two of us got on the raft it might sink too deep and get stuck on the rocks."

So it was arranged, and a few minutes later Dick set off. Peter Marley had cut for him a slender but tough pole, which he was to use in shoving the novel craft across the stream.

"Don't go overboard!" cried Sam.

"I'm going to take off the most of my clothing," answered the older brother. "You can carry the things for meand don't drop them at the ford."

Soon Dick was on the way, standing behind the biplane and using the long pole as best he could. He was in water up to his ankles and as the planks were slippery he had to watch his footing. Once he came close to going overboard but saved himself by clutching one of the wire stays of the machine.

In the middle of the stream the current caught the raft and forced it down the river for quite a distance. But Dick had expected this, and kept his eyes on a sandy stretch still further below. He poled along with vigor, and did what he could to avoid the rocks and shallows. Once the raft caught fast, but soon he had it loose again, and a few minutes later the sandy stretch was gained and he sent the raft shoreward with all his force. It came up on the sand and there it stuck; and the voyage was at an end. Somewhat out of breath, Dick sat down to await the coming of the others.

"Safe and sound, eh?" cried Tom, as he galloped up from the ford. "Good enough!"

"Now what's the next move?" asked Sam, who was at his brother's heels.

"We'll let the horses pull the whole concern up into the meadow," answered Dick. And as soon as Peter Marley arrived this was done, and then the biplane was unfastened from the raft and rolled still further inland, to a level, grassy field belonging to a farm of the vicinity.

The boys were anxious to learn if the engine of the flying machine was in running order, and all set to work at once, drying and cleaning the parts. Fortunately the gasoline tank had remained airtight. While Tom looked over the spark plugs and Sam tried the oil feed, Dick adjusted the carburetor and magneto.

"Now I guess we can try it," said the eldest Rover boy, at last. "But we'll tie her down first," he added, with a grin.

"Yes, and good and hard this time," added Tom.

"Rope her to the raft," suggested Sam. "And drive a few stakes in the ground, too," and this was done.

It was a wonder that none of the propeller blades had been broken, yet such was a fact. They were scratched and nicked, but a coat of varnish would soon remedy all that.

Dick turned on the spark, adjusted the gasoline feed, and then he and Tom took hold of the propeller blades. Half a dozen turns proved unavailing and the boys looked glumly at each other. Had the engine been damaged after all?

"Give her another," said Dick, and this was done. Then the engine suddenly responded, and there followed those gatlinggun like explosions that set the horses to prancing wildly.

"Hi! hi! let up with thet racket!" yelled Peter Marley. "If ye don't them hosses will run away!"

"All right, I'll stop her and you can take the horses up into the field," answered Dick.

He sprang to the front of the biplane to stop the engine, but ere he could do so one of the horses broke away and galloped madly away in the direction of the woods. Then another followed.

"There they go!" bawled the farmer, lustily. "Stop 'em!"

Sam and Tom leaped to do as bidden. But they were too late, and so was Peter Marley. Across the field dashed the horses, badly frightened by the noise, and in a few seconds they disappeared into the timber.

"Well, by gum! Now what's to be did?" asked the farmer helplessly.

"Let's go after 'em!" answered Tom, running for the horse he had ridden. "We ought to be able to catch them, Mr. Marley. Dick and Sam can stay here."

"All right, we'll try it," answered the farmer. "But them critters is powerful runners, I can tell ye thet! That black don't like no better fun than to run away."

"Take care of yourself, Tom," called Dick, who had now stopped the engine. And then he and Sam watched their brother and the farmer as they went riding away at top speed after the runaway steeds.

"Well, anyway, the engine seems to be O. K.," remarked Sam, after the others had disappeared. "And the propellers go around like circular saws. Now all we've got to do is to have those bamboo sticks bound up, or replaced by new ones. Wouldn't it be great if we could go home in this machine!" he added, enthusiastically.

The boys inspected the split poles and the canvas, which had been punctured in several places, and then tried the engine once more.

"Makes a lot of noise," was Sam's comment. "You'd think it was half a dozen Fourths of July rolled into one."

Presently they saw a farmer approaching, accompanied by two boys. The farmer had a shotgun in his hands, and each of the boys carried a club.

"Wot's this noise about, an' wot's that thing?" demanded the farmer, and he showed his nervousness by the way he handled his gun.

"This is an airship," answered Dick, pleasantly. "I was trying the engine, that's all."

"Gosh all hemlock! An airship, eh? I thought it was a company o' soldiers firin' their rifles! Wot be you a'doin' here in my pasture lot?"

"Is this your lot?"

"It sure is, an' has been for forty years."

"We came here with Mr. Marley, of Rayville, to get the machine. It got away from us and landed in the river. We dragged it over here," explained Dick. "We'll make it right with you for using the lot," he added, with a smile.

"Oh, so thet's it, eh? Well, you're welcome to use the lot," said John Snubble. "I'm glad o' the chanct to see an airship. Boys, this is one of them airships you read about in the papers," he went on to his two sons. "Ain't no danger o' an explosion, is there?" he asked anxiously, as he slowly drew closer.

"I don't think so," answered Dick. And then he explained to Mr. Snubble how the two horses had become frightened and run away, and how Mr. Marley and Tom had gone after the runaway steeds.

"It's too bad it's broke," said one of the farmer's sons. "I'd like to see her go up."

"So would I," added the other.

"Perhaps you'll see her go up when she's mended," said Sam.

"If this is your farm, could you rent me a shed in which to store this biplane until she is mended?" said Dick, to the farmer.

"Maybe I can," was the slow answer. "But we'd have to keep the thing out o' sight o' the hosses an' cattle, or they'd cut up wuss nor them hoses did wot run away," the man added soberly.

45

CHAPTER VIII

TRIAL FLIGHTS

It was a full hour before Tom and Peter Marley came back and even then they did not bring the runaway horses in the field where the biplane was located.

"Won't take no more chances," said the farmer. "I kin tie 'em down here on the edge o' the woods jest as well." And this was done.

"Well, we may as well store the machine here for the present," said Dick. "We'll have to get some piano wire for those broken poles."

"Aren't you going to try to take it home?" asked Tom, in surprise.

"What's the use? This is a good field to fly from. We can mend the Dartaway here and then, if Captain Colby is willing, he can sail her from here to our farm."

A big wagon shed was cleaned out, and John Snubble and his sons aided the others in rolling the biplane under the roof. Some old blankets were thrown over the engine.

"Do you think she'd be safe here?" whispered Dick, to Peter Marley.

"She will be so far as Snubble is concerned," said the farmer. "He'll leave her alone, an' so will his sons. But some outsider may come an' fool with her."

"Well, we've got to take that chance," returned the eldest Rover boy. "We won't leave the biplane here any longer than necessary."

It was not until nearly supper time that the boys got back to Rayville. Here Peter Marley was paid for what he had done, and then the youths lost no time in running out their automobile and going home.

The next day they telegraphed to the aviator who was to give them lessons in sailing the Dartaway, and he came as soon as he could. He listened with much interest to what the lads had to tell him.

"Well, it was certainly a great tryout!" he declared. "It proves that the Dartaway is a wellbalanced machine, and that means much."

He had brought with him the necessary wire for repairs, and soon all were on the way to the Snubble farm, taking a road that would land them directly at the door.

"Glad you come!" cried John Snubble on seeing the boys. "Going to take the machine right away, ain't you?"

"We hope to," answered Dick. "Why?" For he saw that the farmer had something on his mind.

"Might have been burnt up last night, that's why."

"Burnt up!" cried Tom. "How?"

"Heard a noise outside about eleven o'clockmy wife did, she ain't well an' don't sleep good. I came down with my shotgun, thinkin' chicken thieves might be around. I heard somebuddy at the flyin' machine and sneaked up to see who it was. Hang my skin if a young feller wasn't there with a lighted candle an' some loose hay, and wantin' to start a fire close to the gasoline tank! I gave a yell, an' he dropped the candle and legged it for dear life."

"Why didn't you stop him, or shoot him?" queried Sam.

"I was too excited, fer the candle dropped into the hay an' it begun to blaze up. I stamped the fire out, an' by that time the feller was out o' sight."

"He must have wanted to blow the biplane up!" exclaimed Captain Colby.

"He sure did, an' he might have burnt up the shed an' the barn, an' the house, too!" added John Snubble.

The three Rover boys looked at each other. The same thought was in the mind of each.

"Tad Sobber!" murmured Sam.

"Sure as you're a foot high," added Tom. "Oh, what a mean thing to do!"

"He must have watched what we did, and then planned to wreck the Dartaway," said Dick. "It's just like his meanness."

"Let's go down to the old mill after him," burst out Tom. "I'd like nothing better than to wipe up the ground with him." And he clenched his fists tightly.

"Humph! Do you think he'd show himself?" asked Sam. "Not much! He'd hide where you couldn't find him. Now he and old Crabtree know we are around they'll take good care not to get caught."

"We might burn down the old mill!" murmured Tom. "It would serve 'em right, for all their meanness."

"Let it go," was Dick's advice. "Some day we'll catch both of them redhanded at something, and then we can give 'em what's coming to 'em."

The matter was talked over with John Snubble and the aviator, and the farmer said he would keep on guard against Sobber and Crabtree and report to Dick if he found out anything unusual. Then the biplane was brought forth, and Captain Colby made an examination.

"All these breaks can easily be mended," said the aviator. "We'll go to work at once. Then I'll give the Dartaway a little tryout, and if she runs as she should I'll take her back to your home."

"Don't you want a passenger?" asked Sam and Tom in a breath.

"Why, do you want to go?"

"Sure!"

"I'm afraid I'll have to disappoint you. I want to try the machine several times before I risk taking anybody up."

The Snubble boys were delighted to think they could see the Dartaway fly and they assisted the others in making the necessary repairs. For two hours all were very busy and then Captain Colby announced the biplane in as good a condition as before the wild flight.

"Now I'll give her a short tryout," he said, and this was done. Up into the air mounted the Dartaway as gracefully as a bird, and all of the boys clapped their hands in delight.

"By gum! beats the nation!" said one of the Snubble lads.

"It's grand! I'm going to save up for one!" added the other.

Around the field sailed Captain Colby and then made the figure eight three times. Then he came down near the spot from which he had started.

"Couldn't be better," he declared. "I could take her a hundred miles if I wished."

"Wish I could go up," said Sam wistfully.

"Your time will come pretty soon," added the aviator. "The flight to your home will be a good test."

A little later the aviator arose again in the air, this time headed for Valley Brook farm. The boys were also ready and started off immediately in the automobile.

"Come again!" shouted the Snubble boys.

"We will," answered Dick. "Your field makes a dandy landing place."

Dick ran the automobile and put on good speed all the way home. As they went along they watched the flight of the biplane, but soon the machine passed from view.

"She certainly can sail!" cried Tom. "Oh, Dick, we'll have to take her to Brill with us!"

"That's it!" cried Sam. "What's the use of leaving her behind? We can sail after college hours."

"Yes, and think how quickly we could get over to Hope Seminary," went on Tom. The place he mentioned was a young ladies' boarding school located not many miles from Brill. Dora Stanhope went to Hope, and so did the two Laning girls.

"We'll see about it," replied Dick, briefly. But the idea of taking the flying machine to Brill pleased him as much as it did his brothers.

When they got home they found that Captain Colby had already arrived. He and the Dartaway were in the field back of the barn, and surrounding the aviator were all the members of the Rover household.

"Well, boys, got back, eh?" cried Anderson Rover, as they rolled up in the automobile.

"Hello, dad!" came from all three. And then they leaped to the ground to greet their parent. All could not help but notice that he looked a trifle pale and careworn.

"Was your trip a success?" asked Dick, in a low voice.

"I don't know yetI hope so," answered the father. "Some business matters have gotten pretty well twisted up. But never mind now. I see your new machine can fly." And Anderson Rover smiled.

"Oh, she's a peach!" cried Tom slangily. "We expect to have the greatest times ever in her!"

"Yes, but you must learn all about the biplane first," added the fond father anxiously. "You mustn't think of going up until you are sure of what you are doing."

"Dat am suttenly de greatest bird wot I most eber see!" declared Aleck Pop solemnly. "If I hadn't dun see it wid my own eyes I wouldn't nebber believe it nohow!"

"That's a fact," added Jack Ness. "When the boys go up in it there won't be no holdin' 'em in."

"We're going to take you up, first thing, Jack," said Tom, with a wink at his brothers.

"Me? Not much!" cried the hired man. "I wasn't built to fly, not me!" And he began to back away in alarm.

After dinner Captain Colby made another trial flight, and then gave the three boys a lesson in the manipulation of the biplane, showing them just how to regulate the engine while running, how to balance the machine, how to steer, and how to make various turns.

"Do you ride bicycles?" he asked.

"We do, and have for years," answered Dick.

"And do you swim?"

"Of course," came from all of the lads.

"Then just remember how you felt when you first tried to ride a wheel and when you first tried to swim. You got excited, didn't you? And when you thought the wheel was going over you gave it a wild twist that did send you over, and when you thought you were going to drown you thrashed around in a way that only made matters worse. Well, that's a lesson to remember in running a flying machine. Don't get excited and lose your presence of mind, or it may cost you your life. Keep cool, act quickly, but don't overdo a thing. If the machine is tipping a little to one side, don't get excited and throw it clean over the other way. And don't try to make any sharp turns until you know your machine thoroughly."

Then he had them watch him while making several flights close to the ground, and told them exactly what he was going to do. This lasted for two days.

"Running an auto and a bicycle will help you," he said. "But sailing a biplane is, after all, a science in itself. But you'll learnI see that by the way you take hold."

There had been a slight breeze blowing during the third afternoon, but towards sunset this went down, and then the aviator said that Dick might try a short flight, over a cornfield that was close by.

"Don't go too high," he cautioned. "And if you feel the biplane turning over try to jump clear of the engine, so it can't crush you."

It must be confessed that Dick's heart beat loudly as he took his seat in the flying machine. It was one thing to talk about going up and quite another to really fly. He realized the danger far more than did merryhearted Tom, or even Sam. But he was not going to show the white feather.

The engine was started, the others holding the machine back. Dick grasped the steering wheel and put his feet on the pedals.

"All ready?" asked Captain Colby.

"Yes. Let go."

"Now be careful. Take it easy,and keep over the cornfield," said the captain. "And if you turn, make a wide circle." He thought a tumble among the corn might not be as bad as one in an open field where the ground was hard.

Those on the ground let go, and with a rush and a whirr the Dartaway sped forward over the ground. Then Dick shifted the elevation rudder, and up into the air rushed the biplane, gathering speed at every revolution of the propellers.

51

The eldest Rover boy was in the air at last!

CHAPTER IX

THE NEW ARRIVAL

"Say, that's great!"

"Be careful, Dick! Don't try too much!"

"He made a very good start," came from Captain Colby, who was watching the progress of the biplane closely.

Over the cornfield sailed the Dartaway with Dick Rover the sole occupant. He was up about fifty feet in the air and presently he went still higher.

"He's making the turn!" cried Sam. "Just look at him coming around!"

"Here he comes back!" exclaimed Tom. "Hurrah! Who says Dick can't fly? Why, he's flying like a veteran!"

"Very good, so far," murmured Captain Colby. "If only he keeps his wits about him he'll be all right."

"Trust Dick to do that," answered Sam. "He knows what he is doing, every time."

The biplane had now reached a point close to where the three stood in the field. All expected Dick to come down, but he did not. Instead, he made another graceful turn to the left, and started over the cornfield a second time.

"I wish the others could see him," murmured Tom. They had not told the folks in the house about the trial flights for fear of scaring them. Everybody thought the boys would not try to fly for at least a week.

Four times did Dick sail around the cornfield, the last time making such a wide circle that he went directly over the barn and the wagon shed. Then he shut off the engine and glided slowly to earth, coming down in the middle of the field with scarcely a jar.

"By the great clam chowder of Pocahontas!" cried Tom, rushing up and helping him out of the machine. "Dick, it was fine! Couldn't have been better!"

"It was immense!" put in Sam. "You made the turns beautifully."

"It was very well done," added Captain Colby. "If you do as well in the future you will have no cause to fear. As far as you are concerned, I reckon the worst is over."

"How did it feel to be up in the air?" queried Sam.

"Oh, I felt kind of funny in my head for a few seconds," answered the older brother. "But I knew I had to pull myself together and I did. After that it was only a question of watching everything closely."

"Now I guess it's my turn, isn't it?" asked Tom, impatiently.

"If you feel equal to it," answered the captain.

"Sure thing."

Once more the biplane was gotten ready, and with another rush and a whizz the Dartaway shot into the air. For a moment, as the machine wobbled from side to side, it looked as if Tom would have an accident, and his brothers gave a shiver. But then he managed to steady the machine and over the cornfield he flew, and around in a big circle twice. Then he made a still larger turn, well up in the air, and in a few seconds more was sailing over the barn and then over the Rover home!

"Gracious, that's Tom!" murmured Sam. "Always bound to go the limit!"

The noise of the engine caused those in the house to rush out and look at the machine.

"Who is running it, that aviator?" queried Mrs. Rover.

"No, it's Tom," replied her husband.

"Tom!" burst out Anderson Rover. "Impossible! Why he doesn't know enough about it yet."

"He'll be killed!" moaned Mrs. Rover. "Oh, what a daring boy!" And she began to wring her hands in despair.

Over the house flew the biplane, and then made another turn and came back. Then came sudden silence.

"Something is wrong!" cried Anderson Rover. "The engine has stopped working!"

"He's coming down like a bird!" exclaimed Aleck Pop. "Now jess to look at dat!"

As he spoke the biplane glided slowly to the ground, landing near the barn. All rushed to the spot. There sat Tom grinning broadly.

"How was that?" he asked coolly. "Wasn't that a dandy initial flight?"

"Tom! Tom!" cried his aunt. "You'll kill me with your daring! Are you hurt? Did something break?"

"No, I'm not hurt, aunty, and nothing broke," he answered. "Oh, it was immense! I could have stayed up an hour if I had wanted to."

"Very goodvery good indeed!" said Captain Colby. "You took a risk in flying over the house, but as nothing went wrong we won't say anything about that."

"Now it's my turn!" cried Sam.

"Has Dick been up?" queried his father.

"Yes, and he made a splendid flight too," answered Tom. "Oh, dad, your sons are born aviators."

"Perhaps. But, Sam, do be careful! Don't try to fly so high at first," pleaded Anderson Rover.

"I'll be careful, dad," answered his youngest offspring.

All remained in the field to watch the flight of the youngest Rover. Sam was a little pale, but just as determined as his brothers had been to succeed. He looked over the biplane carefully, then took his seat, and told them to start the propellers.

Once more the Dartaway arose, and as it did Mrs. Rover could not repress a shudder, for Sam was very dear to her, because he was her dead sister's youngest child, and she had never had any children of her own.

But her fears were groundless, for Sam sailed over the cornfield just as well as had Dick. He did not fly very high, but he kept in the air nearly ten minutes, which was longer than had either of the others. When he came down he did so with a little bump, but this was not enough to hurt anything.

"It's the best ever!" was Sam's comment, when the others gathered around. "Beats autoing all hollow!"

"Wasn't you scared, Massa Sam?" asked Aleck, who had watched the flight with wildlyrolling eyes.

"Not in the least, Aleck, after once I got started. Just when I went up I had a little chill down my backbone, that's all."

"Glory to heaben! Say, yo' know wot I think? I think dare ain't nuffin wot you Rober boys can't natually do, dat's wot!" And with this comment Aleck shuffled off to his work.

"Every one of you did well," was Captain Colby's comment. He turned to Anderson Rover. "You can be proud of your sons, sir. They handled the machine in splendid shape."

"Yes, but I want you to watch them closely, Captain," answered Mr. Rover. "Teach them all there is to know."

"I'll teach them all I know myself," answered the aviator.

That evening the boys could talk of nothing but aviation, and many were their plans for flights in the Dartaway. All wanted Captain Colby to tell them if the biplane could carry three persons.

"I hardly think so," answered the aviator. "It will carry two, though, that I am sure of."

"Well, if it will carry two men it ought to carry three boys," insisted Sam.

"The best way to find out is to try it," went on the captain. "So long as you run with care, nothing can happen to you because of the extra load. Of course if the weight is too heavy the biplane won't go up, or if it does, it won't stay up."

The following day came a telegraph message from one of the old Putnam Hall pupils, Hans Mueller. He sent word that he would be in that vicinity and would call on the Rovers.

"Good for Hans!" cried Tom, who scented fun. "Maybe we can take him up in the Dartaway."

"Hans would be scared stiff," returned Dick.

"It would take all the starch out of him," said Sam.

"In that case, how could he be scared stiff?" asked Tom, dryly.

It was arranged that Sam should run down to the depot with the auto for the German youth. In the meantime Captain Colby and the other boys got out the Dartaway and prepared for more trial flights. Then Dick went up and remained in the air for twelve minutes, making a number of turns that were very graceful, and taking a little trip over the woods back of the farm.

"It's a sport that can't be beat, Tom," he said, on coming down. "I believe everybody will be getting a flying machine before longjust as folks have been getting autos."

The supply of gasoline had been replenished and the lubricating oil renewed, and then Tom went up. He flew around the cornfield twice, then headed in the direction of Oak Run.

"I guess he has gone off to meet Sam and Hans," said Dick. "I heard the train go through and they must be on the way here by now."

"Your brother certainly takes chances," replied Captain Colby.

"He always did. Tom acts first and thinks afterwards,but he usually comes out on top," added Dick, loyally.

In the meantime Sam had reached the depot at Oak Run just as the train came in. He immediately espied Hans Mueller, dresssuit case in hand, and ran to meet him.

"Hello, Hans, old boy!" he exclaimed. "Glad to see you." And he shook hands cordially.

"Is dot you, Sam?" replied the German youth, who, although he had been in this country quite some time, still found a difficulty in mastering the language. "I vos certainly glad to meet you. How vas der udder poys?"

"Oh, Tom and Dick are first rate. They couldn't come down just now, for they are busy with our new biplane."

"A biplane, eh? Vot is dot, some kind of a sawmill alretty?"

"No, Hans, a flying machine. Hop in, and you'll soon be at the farm and then you can look it over." And Sam led the way to the automobile, threw the dresssuit case in the tonneau, and assisted the German youth to a seat in front.

"A flying machine!" cried Hans, as they started off. "By chimanatics! Vot you poys going to git next?"

"I don't know."

"First you get a houseboat, den an autermobile, den a steam yachts, und bicycles, und now it vos a flying machine. Vot you do mid him, Sam?"

"We are learning to fly."

"Vot! you going up by der sky in him?" cried the German youth, aghast.

"Of courseand you can go up with us too."

"Me? Me go up in a airship? Not on your neckties, Sam Rofer! I got too much regart for my neck alretty yet! Ven I fly I valk on der groundt und do it, yah!"

"Oh, it's dead easy when you know how, Hans."

"Dead, hey? Chust vot I dink, Samput I ton't vonts to pe dead, not chust yet!"

They soon passed over the Swift River and through Dexter's Corners and came out on the highway leading to the farm. Looking up into the sky, Hans suddenly saw something unusual approaching.

"Look, look, Sam!" he bawled. "Vot is dot?"

"Oh, that must be our biplane!" answered Sam. "Yes, it is! Dick or Tom must be running it. Isn't it great, Hans?"

"Du meine zeit!" groaned the German youth. "Of Dick or Dom be in dot he preaks his neck sure! Tole him to come town, Sam!"

Sam did not answer, but slowed up the automobile, to better watch the flight of the biplane. Tom was making a graceful curve, so that he might pass directly over the machine below.

"Hello, Hans!" he cried gaily, and waved his hand, for the noise of the engine drowned out his oral salute. Then with a rush the biplane sailed directly over the automobile.

"Sthop! Ton't hit me!" yelled poor Hans, and badly frightened he ducked his head, although the flying machine was fully twentyfive feet above him.

Then Tom made another wide circle and again approached the automobile. But this time he was sailing lower, and even Sam grew uneasy.

"Go up!" he yelled to his brother, and Tom tried to obey. But for some reason, the biplane refused to respond to the rudder, and with a rush and a roar it came directly for the automobile and its occupants!

CHAPTER X

FUN WITH OLD RICKS

It was a moment of extreme peril. Sam brought the automobile to a stop. Had the roadway been wider he might have sheered to one side, but the highway was too narrow for that, and with a ditch on either side, to carry off rain water, he did not want to take a chance of going over.

"Go pack! Go pack!" shrieked Hans Mueller. He was crouching down, looking with staring eyes through the lowered wind shield of the touring car.

Suddenly Sam acted. While the biplane was still a hundred feet away he threw his lever into the reverse and allowed the gears to connect with the engine. Then the automobile began to move backwards, slowly at first and then faster and faster, as the youngest Rover put on the power.

"He's coming! He's coming! Ve peen busted up in a minit!" roared Hans, who was shaking as with the ague. "Oh, vy tidn't I sthay home ven I come to pay dis visit!"

The biplane had slowed down, for Tom had shut off the engine. But the Dartaway still had headway enough to catch up to the automobile and it came up like some bird of illomen, that made even stouthearted Sam quail. But he stuck to his post, sending the automobile backward as fast as he dared. He knew the roadway behind was straight, so he simply steered by keeping the wheel as it was.

"Tom, Tom, can't you do something?" he yelled. "Turn her aside!"

"I'm trying!" yelled back his brother. "The steering outfit is jammed!"

Backward went the automobile and on and on came the big biplane, until the forward part of the machine was almost over the hood of the touring car.

"Maybe you had better jump out!" cried Sam to Hans.

But even as he spoke there came a sudden snap from the flying machine. A caught wire had released itself. At once the biplane could be steered again, and with a dexterous twist of the wheel and a deflection of one of the tips, Tom brought it around. Over a rail fence it sailed, to land gracefully in the open field beyond. Then Sam stopped the automobile.

"Well!" came from the youngest Rover. And that single word meant a good deal.

"Hope I didn't scare you to death," sang out Tom, as he climbed from his seat. "Hans, did you get heart failure?"

"Oh, Dom! Dom! vot for you do him?" asked the German youth, in a voice he tried in vain to steady. "I dink sure you vos going to cut off our heads off alretty!"

"It was the steering outfit did it," explained Tom. "I'm awfully sorry I scared you. I was scared myself. I was going to fly over you and then go back when all at once I found I couldn't budge the rudders. Then I got alarmed, thinking the machine might turn turtle on me, so I shut off the engine, intending to glide to earth. But I didn't want to glide right into the auto. Sam, it's a good thing you thought to run backwards. If you hadn't there would have been a smashup sure!"

"So dot is der new flying machine," remarked Hans, as he walked into the field to inspect the Dartaway. "Mine gracious! she vos almost so pig like a house!"

"Want to go up, Hansy, old boy?" queried Tom.

"Not for a dousand tollers, Dom! No, not for a million!"

"You'll like it, Hans, when you get used to it."

"No, sir; nixy!" returned the German youth firmly. "I sthay py der ground on. You fellers can fly und I vatch you, yah!"

"How are you going to get the machine back?" asked Sam.

"Sail her back," answered his brother promptly. "But I'll have to look at that steering apparatus firstand you'll have to help me start."

"Better let Captain Colby inspect it first," advised Sam.

But Tom did not want to wait, and so he and his brother looked over the flying machine and soon found out what had gone wrong, and fixed it, so that the same accident might not occur again. Then Tom got in, and Sam and Hans started the propellers, and away sailed the youth in a manner that made the German lad stare in amazement.

"Dot's fine!" was Hans's comment. "Say, Dom, he peen a regular aviadventurer, hey?"

"What's that, Hans?"

"Dom, he peen a regular aviadventurer, or vot you call him?"

"Oh, you mean aviator."

"Yah, dot's him. He peen von sure!"

"Your word was O. K., Hans," was Sam's comment. "Tom is certainly an air adventurer!"

The two boys got into the automobile once more and were soon at the Rover homestead, where Hans was warmly greeted by the others, all but Captain Colby knowing him well. Tom had already arrived and the captain was inspecting the biplane with care.

"Such things will happen, especially with a new and stiff machine," said the old aviator. "All you can do is to watch out, and look over the machine with care every time you plan a flight."

Hans had much news of interest to tell about the boys who were still at Putnam Hall and about Captain Putnam and George Strong, the head teacher. He had also seen Mr. and Mrs. Laning, the parents of Nellie and Grace, and had heard something of the latest trouble with Tad Sobber and Josiah Crabtree.

"Vy ton't you got dem arrested?" he asked, when he was told that the evildisposed pair were in that vicinity.

"We don't want the notoriety," said Dick. "If we had them locked up they'd be sure to drag Mrs. Stanhope and the girls into court. We are willing to let them alone if they will only let us alone."

Captain Colby remained at the farm a week and during that time gave the Rover boys as much instruction as possible in the art of flying in general and the art of managing the biplane in particular. He had brought with him several books on flying and recommended that these be read carefully.

"You all seem to take to it naturally," he said. "I don't believe you'll have any trouble excepting on rare occasionsand every person who goes up is bound to have that."

After the captain left the boys took several flights, some of them quite long. They sailed over Dexter's Corners and the railroad station of Oak Run, and at the latter place nearly scared old Ricks, the stationmaster, into a fit, by swooping down close to where he was standing. Dick also made a flight to the Marley place, and visited the Snubble homestead.

"What did you find out?" asked Sam, when he came back from the lastnamed trip.

"Sobber and Crabtree have left the old mill," answered Dick. "The Snubble boys were over there twice and they couldn't see a sign of anybody."

"Have they any idea where they went to?" asked Tom.

"No. They said Crabtree sold the mill property."

"Besser you look out for dem scalavags," was the advice from Hans. "I vouldn't drust dem mit mine eyes open alretty!"

"Oh, we're on the watch!" declared Tom.

The next day the German youth had to leave, and all the boys went down to the railroad station in the touring car to see him off. Old Ricks was there and he glared souring at the Rovers when he saw them.

"I guess he didn't like that flying affair," was Sam's comment.

"Oh, he's thinking of the time Tom put the cannon cracker in the bonfire and made him think some dynamite had gone off," returned Dick, with a grin.

"Or the time Tom gave him the cigar that turned into a snake!" went on Sam, with a laugh.

"Get out of the way! Get out of the way, you boys!" cried the old stationmaster, as he brushed past, hitting Tom in the knee with a suit case he was carrying. The train that carried Hans had rolled away, leaving Ricks and the Rovers alone on the little platform.

"Why, Mr. Ricks, what's your rush?" asked Tom, sweetly. "Going to a wedding?"

"No, I ain't going to no wedding!" grunted old Ricks. "I don't want you young fellers to git in my way, that's all."

63

"Maybe you have to testify in that case in court," went on Tom, with a wink at his brother.

"Ain't got to testify in no court."

"Why, you're in that caseI read all about it in the papers!" cried Tom.

"Me in a case in court?" asked old Ricks, suspiciously.

"Sure. It was a terrible trouble, wasn't it?" went on Tom. "I am mighty sorry for you, really I am, Mr. Ricks."

Now as it chanced, Mr. Ricks had had some trouble with a neighbor over a fence that had blown down between the two properties. The neighbor had threatened to sue him if he did not put the fence up again. The Rovers knew nothing about this, but it had been in old Ricks's mind for a week.

"If anybody sues me he'll git the wust of it!" growled the stationmaster savagely.

"It's a terrible mess, that's a fact," went on Tom. "The papers said he had threatened to get after you with a shotgun!"

"A shotgun? After me?" exclaimed old Ricks, and turned slightly pale.

"And they say you poisoned the cat," put in Dick.

"And caught the dog and starved the poor animal to death," added Sam.

"It ain't soI never teched his cat, nor his dog nuther!" roared old Ricks. "He's a blamed fool, he is!"

"Hush! hush!" whispered Tom, solemnly. "Don't speak so harshly of the dead."

"Dead!" exclaimed the startled Ricks. "Who's dead?"

"Didn't you know he was found on the railroad tracks dead?" asked the funloving Rover. "Of course they say you let the freight train run over him. But we know you wouldn't be so wicked, Mr. Ricks."

"Dead? On the tracks? Me let the train run over him?" halfwhispered the stationmaster. "IIdidn't do it! Say, this is awful! Who told you this?"

64

"Haven't you read the newspapers?" asked Dick.

"That comes for being too stingy to buy a morning paper," added Sam.

"Of course the local papers didn't dare to print the truth," said Tom. "But you'll find a full account in the New York Blizzard and the Philadelphia Bazoo. Your picture on the front page, too, entitled, 'Did He Do It, or Did He Did It Not.'"

"Say, I ain't done nuthin', I tell ye!" almost shouted old Ricks, who was too excited to realize that the boys were making fun of him. "If them blamed city newspapers say I did I'll sue 'em fer damages, that's wot I'll do. I ain't teched Ham Ludd, nor his cat, nor his dog nuther! And it was the wind blew the fence down, I didn't tech that nuther!" He paused to catch his breath, "Where was Ham killed? I didn't hear of anybuddy gitting struck by a train."

"Oh, I don't know who the man was, or where he was struck," answered Tom, as he started to walk away. "But they are after you, Mr. Ricks. If I was you, I'd pack my valise and hike for California, or Sing Sing, or some other place."

"I ain't going to run away, Tom Rover, and you can't make me," was the wild reply. "I ain't teched Ham, nor his cat, nor his dog, nor the fence nuther, I tell ye! It's an outrage to say so! I'll sue them newspapers fer a million dollars damages!"

"I'd make it two millions," answered Tom, calmly, and then started for the automobile, followed by his brothers.

"But see here," went on the stationmaster. "I want to know"

"Sorry, but we haven't time now," put in Dick. "Hurry, Tom!" he whispered.

"It's Ham Ludd coming!" added Sam. "Let's get outbefore the fat's in the fire!"

And off the three Rover boys ran to the automobile and were soon rolling away from the railroad station. But they did not go far.

"I'm going back and watch the fun," said Tom, and leaped out, and ran up behind the station, while his brothers followed him.

CHAPTER XI

OFF FOR BRILL COLLEGE

When old Ricks saw his neighbor approaching he could not at first believe his eyes. Then he ran up to the man, who was a particularly sour individual.

"Say, I thought you was dead," he gasped.

"Dead?" returned Ham Ludd. "Do I look like I was dead?" And he glared savagely at Ricks. "I ain't dead, not by a jugful!"

"Humph! Well, if you ain't dead, mebbe you'll explain about that cat, an' dog," went on old Ricks.

"Wot about 'em?"

"You told folks I poisoned the cat and starved the dog to death."

"I did not."

"You didit was in the newspapers!" bawled old Ricks, commencing to dance around.

"I didn't! Where's them newspapers?" asked Ham Ludd, also growing excited.

"I ain't got 'em, but Tom Rover said"

And then suddenly old Ricks stopped short. He was commencing to "smell a mouse," as the saying is.

"Wot did Tom Rover say?" demanded Ham Ludd.

"Never mind wot he said," grumbled the stationmaster. "Only you be careful o' wot you say about me in the future, Ham Ludd, thet's all!"

"Huh! I guess that Rover boy has been a'jokin' you ag'in, Ricky," said Ludd, with a grin. "How about thet bustedup bonfire, an' that snaky cigar? Ha! ha! he had you them times, didn't he?"

"You shet up, Ham Ludd!" roared the stationmaster. "Don't you say another word!"

"I'll say all I please! An' you'll put up that fence, too, or I'll have the law on ye!" retorted Ham Ludd; and then went on his way.

"Hang them Rover boys anyway!" muttered old Ricks, as he gritted his teeth. "I'll be glad when they go off to college ag'in. Wish they would stay away!" And he went about his work.

"Ricks and Ludd will have it in for each other from now on," remarked Dick, as he and his brothers got into the automobile to go home.

"Yes, and he'll have it in for usme especially," returned Tom, with a broad grin. "Never mind; I can stand it," he added, carelessly. Troubles, past or to come, never set heavily on that funloving youth's shoulders.

The boys had given the biplane one trial in carrying two passengers, Dick and Sam going up together while Captain Colby was present. On the day following the departure of Hans, they rearranged the seats on the Dartaway and got ready to go up three strong, provided the biplane would carry the load.

"I know she will do it if we get a more powerful engine," said Dick.

"Then we'll get the engine," returned Sam.

They made the start with care, all the others at the homestead being present to witness the trial. The Dartaway went up slowly, with Dick in the center, at the wheel, and Sam on one side of him and Tom on the other.

"Hurrah! we are going to make it!" cried Tom, as the biplane arose like some big bird.

"It's a strain though," answered Dick. "We won't be able to fly very high nor very long."

"But it's great to be up together!" murmured Sam.

They flew for nearly ten minutes, making wide circles and a big figure eight. They went over the house and the barn, and in plain sight of several surrounding farms, men, women and children coming out to look at them. Once more the Rover boys were the talk of the whole countryside.

"Ain't nothing they can't do," said one of the farmers living near. "If they tackle a thing it's plumb bound to go through, every time!"

"It's because they are so full of grit and push," answered his wife. "Wish our Jed was like 'em," she added, wistfully.

"Jed ain't never had no chanct, Mirandy."

"Boys like them Rovers make their own chances, Silas," she retorted.

That evening it was Tom who made a proposal that met with instant approval from his brothers.

"Let's go to the college in the biplane," he said.

"Hurrah! just the cream!" returned Sam. "Say, won't the fellows stare when they see us!"

"Very nice, but we can't very well fly all the way from here to Ashton," put in Dick, mentioning the town near which Brill College was located.

"Oh, I didn't mean that," explained Tom. "I meant to fly from Ashton to Brill. We could ship the biplane to Ashton in secret, put it together on the sly, and create a big sensation by coming down right on the college campus."

"Tom, you're a wonder!" cried Sam. "It's the best plan ever! Oh, let's do it!"

"Wonder where we could ship it to, so the other fellows wouldn't get on to what was doing?" mused Dick.

"Why not ship it to Mr. Sanderson?" suggested Sam. The man he mentioned was a farmer living some distance from the college. The boys had once done the farmer's daughter Minnie a great favor, saving her from insults at the hands of Jerry Koswell and Dudd Flockley.

"That's the talk!" cried Tom. "He'll take care of it and let us put it together in one of his open fields. Then we can make the fellows at Brill open their eyes."

The new idea pleased all the youths immensely, and the next day a long letter of explanation was sent to Mr. Sanderson, and he was asked to telegraph a reply. The biplane was taken apart and packed up for transportation, and then the boys packed their trunks and dresssuit cases, and got ready to "go back to the greasy grind," as Tom expressed it.

It must not be supposed that the lads had forgotten to write to the Stanhopes and the Lanings, and to their college friends. Numerous letters had been mailed and about an equal number had been received. The girls were all going to Hope, but one week later than the boys would have to depart for Brill. Nothing more had been seen or heard of Crabtree or Sobber, for which all were thankful.

"Here's a letter from William Philander Tubbs," said Tom. "I sent him a letter just for fun, asking him the style in socks this fall. Listen to his reply." And he read the following:

"I have been making diligent inquiries about the shades in socks, my dearest Thomas, but the storekeepers seem to be a little undecided. Some think that Rambler Red will prevail while others favor Nile Green and a new shade called Baby's Breath. Personally I favor Baby's Breath and have purchased one dozen of that shade. If I get any more definite news about shades I will wire you, because I know what a dreadful thing it is not to have the shade that is really and truly fashionable."

"Three cheers for William Philander and his Baby's Breath socks!" cried Sam. "He's the true and only artist!"

"Baby's Breath!" murmured Tom. "Now wouldn't that get your scalplock?" And then there was a merry laugh all around.

There was likewise a letter from Max Spangler, and another from Stanley Browne, stating they were already on their way to Brill. Then, just before the boys were ready to leave home, came a letter from Songbird Powell.

"I'll bet it's in verse," said Dick. "Songbird couldn't write prose to save his life."

"We'll soon see," said Sam, who held the communication, and he tore it open. "You win," he added, and then read the following, after the date line:

"My dearest boys
I'm filled with joys
To think that we
Together shall be
In a week or more!
Oh, the fun in store!

And also the work
Which we can't shirk
And the pleasant meetings,
And pleasant greetings,"

"He was thinking of Minnie Sanderson when he wrote that," interrupted Tom.

"Sure thing," returned Dick; for all of the Rovers knew that the wouldbe poet was deeply smitten with the farmer's daughter. He had written several poems about her, and had also given her several presents.

"Well, there are twelve pages of the doggerel," said Sam, glancing over the sheets. "Here, you can read over my shoulders," and this was done, amid much merriment. Songbird had but little news and promised to be at college when they arrived.

"Oh, I hope the Dartaway carries us there in good shape," murmured Tom. "It will be an arrival worth remembering!"

Before he left home Dick had a long talk with his father and his Uncle Randolph. When he rejoined his brothers he was unusually sober.

"What is it, dad's business affairs?" queried Sam.

"Yes, Sam."

"Are they in bad shape?" questioned Tom, quickly. "What's gone wrong?"

"It's something about those mining shares that dad and Uncle Randolph invested in," answered Dick. "I'll give you the particulars later. They don't want Aunt Martha to know about it, for it will only make her worry without doing any good. I'm afraid dad and Uncle Randolph are in it bad," went on Dick, soberly.

"Can't something be done?" asked Tom.

"Not just now. Dad is going to Chicago about it next week again."

"Does he and uncle stand to lose much?" questioned Sam.

"Yes, a good dealmore in fact than they can afford."

"Phew! That's too bad!" murmured the youngest Rover, and Tom shook his head soberly, and forgot all about the parting jokes he had intended to play on Aleck Pop and Jack Ness.

At last came the time for the three Rover boys to leave home. The biplane had been shipped to Ashton by express and their trunks and suit cases had been forwarded on their railroad tickets. They were going a day ahead of time, and Mr. Sanderson had agreed to meet them and take them to his home.

"Good bye, my boys," said the fond father, on parting. "Take good care of yourselves."

"We will," they answered as they shook hands.

"Learn all you can," put in Randolph Rover.

"Take care and don't get into trouble," admonished Mrs. Rover, and then she kissed them tenderly.

"Don't forget to let me know how matters go in Chicago, dad," whispered Dick, to his parent.

"I'll remember, my son."

"And if I can aid you in any way, let me do it,even if I have to leave Brill," went on Dick.

"There is nothing to do at present, Dick. I must wait for that report."

Soon the boys were in the touring car, with Jack Ness to bring the automobile back from the railroad station, he now being able to run the machine. Dick was at the wheel. Tom had cranked up, and off they sped, with a merry shout and with those left behind waving their hands.

"Let her go, Dick!" sang out Tom.

"Good bye!" yelled Sam.

"Good bye!" came back faintly from the homestead.

Then a turn of the road shut out the house from view. Once again the Rover boys were off for college. Little did they dream of the strange adventures in store for them.

71

CHAPTER XII

A GRAND ARRIVAL

"Glad to see you, boys! You're looking prime!"

It was the greeting of Mr. Sanderson, as the Rovers stepped from the train at Ashton. The farmer was waiting at the platform with a twoseated carriage to take them to his farm.

"How are you, Mr. Sanderson!" came from the three, and then all continued in a chorus: "Did the biplane get here?"

"Something got heretwo boxes an' several big bundles," answered the farmer. "I had everything carted over to my place."

"Two boxes and four bundles," said Dick.

"Right you are. One of 'em putty heavy, too."

"That was the engine, Mr. Sanderson," vouchsafed Sam.

"Is that so! Well, times are sure changin', an' bymeby the hosses won't be in it no more. So you calkerlate to fly over to the college."

"We do, if we can get the machine into shape," answered Tom. "It may be that something got broke on the way and will have to be mended," he added, anxiously.

"Well, we didn't break anything, Tom, take my word on that. If anything's broke the railroad company done it."

The boys were soon seated in the carriage and Mr. Sanderson took up the reins. As my old readers know, the farmer was proud of his horses and he had good reason to be, for they started off in fine style, and presently were passing everything on that long and somewhat dusty road.

"How is Miss Minnie?" asked Tom, on the way.

"Fust rate, Tom. She went drivin' yesterday with that young feller from Brill that sprouts poetry."

"Oh, then Songbird has really arrived!" cried Tom.

"He has." Mr. Sanderson looked serious for a moment. "Say, is he any goodor is he allwell, all poetry?"

"Songbird is one of the best and smartest boys in the college, Mr. Sanderson," said Dick, bound to put in a good word for their chum. "He likes to make up verses, but that isn't all he can do. Some day he'll be a good business man."

"Well, I'm glad to hear that," answered the farmer; and the three Rover boys knew he was thinking of his only daughter Minnie, and of the attention Songbird Powell was paying to her.

It was not long before they came in sight of the Sanderson homestead, pleasantly located in a grove of trees. Minnie Sanderson was on the lookout for thema roundfaced, jolly young ladyand she waved her hand as the carriage came to a halt.

"Why didn't you come in that wonderful airship!" she sang out gaily. "I'm dying to see you fly!"

"Because you have the machine here!" answered Sam.

"Oh, we've only got some bundles, and they don't look a bit like a flying machine," went on the girl. "But, say," she added, her cheeks dimpling. "What a time I had yesterday, keeping your secret! Mr. Powell took me out riding,"she blushed a trifle"and when we came back he wanted to know what the bundles contained. I told him it was some kind of machinery. He saw the canvas and said he guessed pa was going to put up a windmill!"

"Thanks for keeping it dark!" cried Dick. "We want to surprise everybody at Brill."

"You'll have to be careful of what you do then," went on the girl. "Some of the young men have been around, and Iwell, I don't like it."

"Who was around?" asked Tom.

"Mr. Flockley, for one," and Minnie bit her lip, for she had not forgotten how that dudish collegian had once insulted her,the time the Rover boys had come to her rescue, as related in detail in "The Rover Boys at College."

"Did he come to the house?" asked Sam.

"Oh, no, he merely walked through the orchard. But I guess he saw some of the packages."

"He didn't speak to you, did he?" asked Dick, bluntly.

"I didn't give him the chance. When I saw him, I walked into the house, and he didn't dare to follow me."

It was almost supper time, and the boys had arranged to remain at the Sanderson homestead, instead of going to the rather poor hotel at Ashton. They had a merry time with the others over the repast, and then, even though it was late, they went down to the barn to inspect the boxes and bundles comprising the Dartaway.

"Everything seems to be all right," said Dick. "We ought to be able to put her together in a day, if we all work hard enough."

"We'll get up at six in the morning," said Sam.

So it was arranged, and Mr. Sanderson said he would call them. But this was unnecessary, for all were up and downstairs before the appointed hour, and before breakfast was served they had the boxes and bundles open and the various portions of the biplane ready for assembling.

"Can't I help?" asked the farmer, who was much interested in what was going on.

"You can help us lift the engine," said Dick. "That is rather heavy."

The boys and the farmer worked until five o'clock in the afternoon over the biplane, knocking off a half hour for dinner. For that meal they had same fried chicken and fresh vegetables, and an apple pie made by Minnie which Tom declared was "a dream."

"We'll come and board with you," said Dick, to the girl. "This sort of food goes away ahead of the college stuff; eh, boys?"

"Indeed it does!" cried Tom.

"Can't be beaten," put in Sam. And these compliments pleased the farmer's daughter very much.

Gasoline was at hand and also oil, and soon the youths had the engine of the biplane in working order. But it was not started until the Dartaway had been rolled off to the middle of a big field.

"I don't want to scare your horses and cattle," explained Dick, to the farmer. "When the engine starts they'll think Fourth of July has arrived."

Soon all was in readiness, and with a final inspection of the biplane, Dick took his seat in the machine and called to his brothers to work the propellers. Bang! bang! bang! went the cylinders, and around went the big blades, faster and faster, until only a blur could be seen. Then over the field shot the Dartaway and up in the air.

"Oh, my, just to look at that!" gasped Minnie. "Just like a big bird!"

"Well, I'll be switched!" cried Mr. Sanderson. "An airship, sure as you are born! I didn't think I'd live to see one! My! my! just to see that thing asailin' through the air!"

Dick made the circuit of the field and then cut a figure eight. The machine seemed to work perfectly, and when he came down he was well satisfied.

"All aboard for Brill College!" he cried. "Through passage only! No stopovers allowed!"

"Shall we sail over now, or wait until tomorrow?" asked Sam.

"Oh, come on now!" cried Tom, impatiently. "Lots of fellows will be on the campus at this hour, and we can do some circling around before we land."

"I'm willing," said Dick. "Who is to do the steering?"

"You do it—you're the oldest," said Sam.

"That's right," added Tom.

"I don't want all the glory," insisted Dick.

"You are not going to have," went on the funloving Rover. "See what I've got for Sam and myself." And he brought out a mysterious package he had brought from home. It contained two silken American flags and two tin horns.

"We'll do the patriotic while you run the machine," said Sam.

"And I've got something elsebut never mind what it is," went on Tom.

"No fireworks, Tomthey are too dangerous in a flying machine," warned Dick, who knew his brother's love for things that made a noise.

"Nothing dangerous this time, Dick, I'll give you my word."

The Dartaway was given another inspection and then staked to the ground with a strong rope, fastened by a slip knot. Then the engine was started up and the three lads clambered on board.

"Good bye!" they cried to the Sandersons.

"Good bye and good luck!" answered the farmer.

"Let us know how you arrive," added his daughter.

Then the knot in the rope was allowed to slide, and with a rush and a whizz the biplane sped over the smooth ground and then soared into the air. By the time Sam had hauled in the dangling rope, the flying machine had left the Sanderson farm far behind.

"Oh, this is simply glorious!" cried Tom. He had his flag in one hand and his horn in the other, and Sam was similarly equipped.

"Of course you know the way, Dick," said the youngest Rover.

"Oh, yes, it's easy. I'll simply follow the road. But I am going up a bit," added Dick. "I don't want to scare any horses, or we may have some damage suits to settle."

"The horses will have to get used to flying machines, just as they had to get used to autos," was Sam's comment.

On and on flew the Dartaway, Dick managing the biplane as skillfully as if he was a seasoned aviator. Over the farms and barns and houses they sailed, creating much astonishment. The inhabitants came rushing forth, some with milk pails, and women with dish cloths and towels in their hands. One boy in his excitement shied a dipper at them, the object falling short of its mark by several hundred yards.

"We are waking folks up," remarked Tom, as he tooted his horn and waved his flag, and Sam followed suit. Then the funloving Rover placed his horn under his arm and began to fumble at something in his pocket.

"I see Brill!" cried Sam, presently. "There is the main building!" And he pointed with his hand.

"I see it," answered Dick. "Now for a few circles and a figure eight before we come down. I hope they'll give us room to land."

In a few seconds more the various buildings belonging to the institution of learning were in full view. Dick started up the engine with renewed speed, thereby making more noise, and Tom and Sam added to the din by blowing the horns with all their might. The two boys also waved the flags.

The racket had the desired effect. From one building and another ran the students and the members of the faculty, and also the hired help, and all gazed up into the sky to learn what the noise meant.

"It's an airship!"

"There are three people on board!"

"Say, doesn't she sail along beautifully!"

"Wonder if they are sailing across the state."

"Maybe they are in the oceantoocean race."

"They look like three boys! See, two of them are waving flags! Now what do you think of that!"

"I'm going to get my spyglass," said one of the under teachers, and ran to do so. In the meantime the Dartaway came closer and circled slowly over the main college building and the broad campus.

"THREE CHEERS FOR THE ROVER BOYS!" CALLED OUT ONE OF THE SENIORS. "Look! look!" cried several of the students. "What are they up to?"

77

From the bottom of the craft had suddenly burst a cluster of red, white and blue tissuepaper streamers. These floated under and behind the Dartaway, producing a beautiful effect. Then suddenly came floating down through the air a quantity of manycolored confettitiny bits of pretty paper that settled everywhere.

"The Rover boys!" cried the teacher who had brought out his spyglass. "They are the three Rover boys!"

"The Rover boys!" cried Songbird Powell, who stood near. "Are you sure?"

"Yes."

"Hurrah!" shouted Stanley Browne. "Now, isn't that just like them? Always up to something new and original."

"Three cheers for the Rover boys!" called out one of the seniors. And the cheers were given with a will, while the Dartaway continued for some time to float over the college grounds and then came settling down like some big white bird, in the very center of the campus.

CHAPTER XIII

SOME INTERESTING NEWS

Before the biplane had come to a complete standstill the students on the campus made a rush and surrounded the three Rover boys.

"The grandest arrival I ever heard of!" cried Songbird Powell, as he caught one after another by the hand. "I shall have to write some verses about this."

"However did you manage it?" queried Stanley Browne. "I didn't know you could run an aeroplane."

"It's out of sight alretty!" came from Max Spangler. "But we could see it, yes!" he added hastily.

"Oh, we thought we'd give the fellows a little surprise," answered Dick modestly. "We purchased the biplane some time ago. It's easy to run after you get the knack of it."

"But carrying three!" went on Stanley. "I've heard of 'em carrying two but not more than that."

"It's quite a load," said Tom. "We've got to have a more powerful engine if we want to carry that many right along."

"And the streamers and confetti!" cried Songbird. "I'll bet those were Tom's idea!"

"You're right," answered Dick.

"And he thought of the flags and horns, too," put in Sam, bound to place the credit where it was due.

"I had to do something to let off steam," said Tom lightly. "Dick wouldn't allow me to fire a bomb, or a cannon, or anything like that," he continued dryly.

During this talk many of the students and instructors commenced to inspect the biplane, and soon the Rover boys were kept busy answering questions.

"Well, young gentlemen, allow me to congratulate you on your successful flight to this place!" said a pleasant voice, and turning the youths found themselves confronted by Doctor John Wallington, the head of the college. He smiled broadly as he shook hands. "This surely marks an epoch in the history of Brill," he went on. "First arrival of students by airship," and he turned to Professor Blackie, who was with him.

"You are right, sir," returned that instructor. "We'll have to make a note of it." And this was done; and anybody going to Brill can see the record in the "history book" of that famous institution.

"Look who's here!" suddenly cried a cheery voice, and Will Jackson, usually called "Spud," because of his liking for potatoes, pushed his way to the Rover boys' side. "I was upstairs dressing when you arrived, but I saw it all from the window. Say, that flight couldn't be beaten. You must have come about three miles a minute, eh? Puts me in mind of the time I was caught in a Kansas cyclone. The wind carried me off my feet, and landed me high up on the side of a big building, and there I had to stick until the wind went down! Fact, and if you don't believe it, some day I'll show you one of the bricks from that same building. I keep it to sharpen my penknife on."

"The same old Spud!" cried Dick, while the others laughed outright. "Telling a yarn before he even shakes hands. How are you?" And he gave Will's hand a squeeze that made the storyteller wince.

"We'll have to have some place in which to store the biplane," said Sam to Dr. Wallington. "Do you think we could put it in the boathouse for the presentor in the shed of the gymnasium?"

"You may use the gymnasium shed, if you can get the machine inside," replied the head of the college. "I presume we'll have to build regular hangars here,if the students are going to own flying machines," he added, with a smile.

"Well, they are good advertisements, Doctor," put in Tom. "Nothing like being uptodate, you know."

"Perhaps, Rover, perhaps. And it will be instructive to all here, to watch you and your brothers manipulate the biplane. But do not let the use of the machine interfere with your studies."

"Oh, we'll use it like we would our bicycles, or a motor boat, or an auto," said Sam. "We came back to make a record for ourselves."

"I am glad to hear it, Samuel, very glad indeed." And then the good doctor hurried away to attend to his official duties.

Some of the late arrivals wanted the Rover boys to give another exhibition flight, and for their benefit Tom took a little sail by himself, and then Sam went up for five minutes. Then the biplane was rolled over to the big shed attached to the gymnasium,a place usually used for housing carriages and automobiles during athletic contests. Here one end was cleaned out and the Dartaway was rolled in, and the engine was covered with a tarpaulin brought from the boathouse.

During the time that all this was being done, one student of Brill had kept to himself, even though greatly interested in what was going on. This was Dudd Flockley, the dudish youth who had once been the crony of Jerry Koswell and Bart Larkspur. There was a sneer on his handsome face.

"Great work, eh, Dudd?" said Bob Grimes, one of the students, in passing.

"I don't know what you mean," returned Flockley, coolly.

"Oh, yes you do, Dudd," retorted the other. "But I suppose it's sour grapes for you," he added pointedly, for he was a friend to the Rovers and knew something about the troubles of the past.

"Bah!" came from Dudd Flockley, and he turned and hurried away. "Now those Rover boys have come back I suppose they'll try to lord it over everybody, just as they did before. How I hate them! I wish I could do something to get them in a hole!" He had forgotten completely the kindness the Rover boys had shown him, and how they had gone to the head of the college and pleaded for him, so that he had been allowed to remain at Brill. Perhaps Flockley was not as wicked at heart as his former college cronies, Larkspur and Koswell, but he was equally ungrateful.

Soon the Rover boys and their chums were up in the dormitory where they had their rooms. As before, Tom and Sam were together, in Number , with Dick and Songbird in Number , and Stanley and the others not far off.

"Home again!" sang out Tom, as he dropped in an easy chair. "My, but this looks natural!" he added, glancing around.

"I want to tell you something," said Stanley, who had followed the three brothers and Songbird into one of the rooms. "Maybe we'd better shut the door," he added, significantly.

"Yes, he's got news," added Songbird. "Say, it beats the nation how some fellows hold a grudge," he went on.

"What's the trouble now?" demanded Dick, quickly.

"Day before yesterday I was over to Ashton," answered Stanley, after the door to the room had been closed and locked. "I went by the upper road and I had to pass that new roadhouse, the place called the Red Horseshoe. Well, who was sitting on the piazza but Jerry Koswell and Bart Larkspur. They had been having a gay time, I guess, and both were talking loudly. When they saw me they called to me to stop, and then they asked me if you fellows had come back to Brill."

"What did you tell them?" asked Tom.

"I told them no, but that you were expected in a few days. Then both of them began to brag, and said they had it in for all three of you Rovers."

"Did they say what they intended to do?" questioned Tom.

"Not exactly, but Koswell intimated that if you didn't look out you might be blown up."

"Blown up!" exclaimed Dick, and he thought instantly of what Tad Sobber and Josiah Crabtree had said to Dora and Nellie.

"That's what he said. I wanted to find out what he meant, but Larkspur stopped him from talking and told him to shut up. But, Dick, I feel sure they mean something, and all of you fellows better be on your guard," added Stanley earnestly.

"This is surely getting interesting," said Tom. "First Sobber and old Crabtree promise to blow us up and now Koswell and Larkspur propose the same thing."

"They must be in league with each other!" cried Sam.

"It looks that wayespecially after what happened on Casco Bay," returned Dick. And then he told Songbird and Stanley of the recent happenings near the Rovers' home, and elsewhere.

"Well, my advice is, keep your eyes wide open all the time," said Songbird. "Those fellows are desperatetheir actions show itand they'll play you foul if they get half a chance."

"And to that advice let me add something more," said Stanley. "Don't trust Dudd Flockley. He pretended to reform for a while, but behind it all I think he is as bad as ever. If you gave him any information he may carry it straight to those others."

"Thank you, Stanley, I'll remember that," said Dick.

"So will I," added Tom, and Sam nodded in approval.

"Well, to let you in behind the scenes," went on Dick, to Stanley and Songbird, "I am not so much worried about ourselves as I am about Mrs. Stanhope and Dora and the Lanings. Sobber and old Crabtree want that fortune from Treasure Isle the worst way and they'll do anything to get hold of it. Koswell and Larkspur are probably short of funds, and, as they like to live high, they'll help Sobber and Crabtree all they can,for a rakeoff of the proceeds."

"I reckon you are right," said Songbird. "But what do all of them mean by blowing you sky high."

"That remains to be seen," said Sam.

"Or rather felt," added Tom, who had to have his little joke. "Maybe they'll plant some dynamite under the college and blow us up!"

"Hardly that, Tom," returned his older brother. "But they may try some kind of a dirty trick along those lines."

"Don't worry, boys, don't worry!" cried Songbird soothingly. "Let the troubles of the future take care of themselves", and then he murmured softly:

"Though the skies be dark and dreary
And hope be almost dead,
And hearts are all so weary"

"Each one can go to bed!"
finished Tom. "A fine bit of poetry truly, Songbird, old sport."

"Who said anything about going to bed?" snorted the wouldbe poet. "I had a finer line than that, Tom. It waserit wasaera Oh, dear, you've quite driven it out of my head!"

"Never mind, it will come back day after yesterday, or before and sooner," went on the funloving Rover blandly. "Now let us put away our things and get ready for supper. I'm as hungry as a wolf in a famine."

"That's right," chimed in Sam. "Aeroplaning can give one a wonderful appetite."

"It's the air," said Stanley.

That evening, after a good meal, the Rover boys had to tell of their various experiences with the biplane. Not a student of Brill had ever gone up in a flying machine although several had gone up in balloons at county fairs and elsewhere. The Rovers had to promise to take up half a dozen of their chums. So far during the fall, talk of football had filled the air, but now all became flying and flying machines. Several of the richer students promised themselves machines in the near future.

"That's the talk!" cried Tom, enthusiastically. "Then we can have some races!"

"Maybe we can even get up an intercollegiate aeroplaning contest," remarked Sam.

"I'm afraid it's a little too early for that yet," answered Dick. "But such contests may come one of these days."

The Rover boys were tired out from their day of labor and excitement and ten o'clock found them in their rooms ready to go to bed. Tom and Sam had started to take off their shoes when there came a faint tap on the door and Bob Grimes appeared.

"Hello, Bob!" cried Tom. "What can I do for you?"

"Hush! not so loud!" whispered the other student, with a glance over his shoulder down the corridor. "Listen, both of you," he went on hurriedly. "Don't ask me any questions, but if you don't want your biplane ruined be sure and guard it closely!" And having spoken thus, Bob Grimes hurried down the corridor and out of sight.

84

CHAPTER XIV

THE BIRTHDAY FEAST

The two Rover brothers looked at each other in amazement, and for a moment neither spoke.

"What do you suppose he meant?" asked Sam, presently.

"He meant just what he said," returned Tom. "I'm going to tell Dick," and he summoned his big brother without delay.

"I think I can piece this together," said Dick. "I saw Bob Grimes talking to Dudd Flockley this afternoon, and again after supper. Most likely Bob got on the trail of something Dudd thinks of doing. He doesn't want to appear as a tattletale and at the same time he doesn't want to see our machine ruined. So that's why he warned you in such a queer fashion."

"You must be right," answered Tom. "What shall we do?"

"Nothing, Tom."

"Yes, but we don't want the machine ruined, or even tampered with!" exclaimed Sam.

"I don't think anybody will touch it," went on the eldest Rover boy. "After you came up here I got to thinking that maybe Flockley, or Koswell, or Larkspur, or somebody else, might try to injure the Dartaway, and so I went to see Filbury, the janitor, about it. His son Abner is helping him around the dormitories, and I hired Abner for fifty cents a night to sleep in the shed and guard the biplane. Abner has got a shotgun, and he isn't afraid of anybody; so I reckon the Dartaway will be perfectly safe."

"Good for you, Dick!" cried Tom. "Say, I hope if anybody does try to injure the machine Abner gives him a dose of shot!"

"I told him not to shoot anybody unless it was necessary," answered Dick. "But he may shoot into the air, just to scare the intruder and raise an alarm."

The next day was such a busy one for the Rover boys that they had no time to do more than look at the biplane and see that it was safe. Abner Filbury reported that he had

85

slept in a hammock slung beside the machine and that nothing had happened to arouse him. Nobody but the Rovers knew that he was on guard. The boys wanted to tell Bob Grimes, but that individual kept out of the way.

After having settled down in their rooms and to their studies, the three Rover boys made several flights in the biplane, including one to the Sanderson farm, where they discovered Songbird calling on Minnie. Both were seated in a hammock between the house and the barn, and both leaped up in confusion when the biplane, manipulated by Tom, sailed directly over their heads. When the Rovers came down in the big field, Minnie ran to greet them, and, later, she treated them to apple pie and some milk. Then they set sail once more, leaving their college chum to finish his interrupted visit.

After this flight the boys ordered a new engine for the Dartaway, one which would make sailing safer, especially in a stiff wind. The makers said they would send the new engine immediately, and a machinist to install it, and they agreed to take the old engine back at cost price, since it was practically new.

It must not be supposed that the Rover boys neglected their studies. As my old readers know, whatever they tackled they went at with all their might, and this applied to their work as well as to their play.

"Dad sent us here to get an education," said Dick. "And while I am here I am going to study all I can. There is no telling how long I'll be able to remain here anyway."

"Thinking of dad's western affairs?" asked Sam.

"Yes; I may have to take hold and help him and Uncle Randolph out. Both of them are not as young as they used to be, you know."

"That's true, Dick. I noticed dad's hair getting pretty gray, and uncle's is almost white."

The boys had written home and also to the Stanhopes and the Lanings, and soon came letters in return. One, from Mr. Anderson Rover, was of special importance.

"I have news out of the ordinary," wrote the parent. "That man Crabtree and Tad Sobber have come back to the old mill. I got the word from Peter Marley. He says they act very suspiciously, and that a boy who works for him overheard Crabtree and Sobber talking about us. I have sent for a detective to come out from the city and watch them for a while. If anything new develops I will let you know."

"Now what in the world can old Crabtree and Sobber be up to?" asked Sam, after all had read the communication.

"Up to some trick, I'll bet a new hat," declared Tom. "I am glad dad sent for the detective. I hope he catches them redhanded at something, and locks them up."

"They certainly ought to be locked up," was Dick's comment.

The boys studied hard that evening and by ten o'clock all were tired out and ready to go to bed. But, just as they were on the point of retiring, there came a knock on the door of the room occupied by Tom and Sam, and Stanley appeared.

"You are wanted in Room !" said the student, in a loud whisper. "Come right along."

"What's up?" asked both boys.

"Feasticecream and cake. Max and Spud were down to the town and they brought the stuff along. Come on, before it's too late and the icecream melts."

"Me for the icecream!" cried Tom, and did a handspring over his bed. "Are the others invited?"

"Surea round dozen," answered Stanley.

Room was at the end of the corridor and occupied by two students named Lane and Parley, wholesouled fellows who were always ready for a good time. The room was so located that it had much more privacy than the other apartments.

Soon the boys had gathered,as jolly a crowd as could be found at Brill. Max and Spud had spread themselves, it being the GermanAmerican lad's birthday.

"Say, this is certainly fine!" cried Sam, as he surveyed several big cakes, two hands of bananas, some grapes, and several bricks of icecream of various flavors.

"How are you going to serve the icecream?" asked Dick.

"Oh, we're all prepared!" cried Spud, and exhibited a "nest" of paper saucers and another of paper plates, and then a handful of tin spoons. "I thought these would answer better than the real thing, for when we have finished we won't have to wash anythingwe can throw the whole mess away."

"Say, that's Spud," cried the student named Lane. "Once he had to wash dishes at a picnic we went to and you ought to see the face he cut."

"Come, git busy alretty!" cried Max, as he flourished a knife and commenced to cut one of the cakes. "Spud, chop the icecream up right avay!"

"All right, me for the chopping!" cried Spud cheerfully, and soon the cream was being passed around to the assembled students, and the cake and fruit followed.

"Fine!" cried Tom, as he smacked his lips over the feast. "Max, you have my full permission to have a birthday once a week."

"Yes, and when you miss a week let Spud take your place," added Sam.

"One thing I can't understand, Spud," said Dick, with great seriousness, and everybody present stopped eating to hear what the eldest Rover might have to say.

"What can't you understand?" asked Spud innocently.

"How you could get up a feast like this and forget to supply such an important thing."

"What important thing?" demanded Spud, and he suddenly looked a trifle worried.

"Potatoes," returned Dick.

For an instant there was silence, and then, as the other boys remembered Will's love of potatoesa love that had given him the nickname of "Spud," there was a wild burst of laughter.

"Say, Spud, that's one on you!"

"Too bad we didn't bring a few praties along, son!"

"We might have fried a few over the light, eh?"

"Don't you worry, dis feast ain't done yet alretty!" cried Max. "Here is something more!" And going to his bureau he brought out a square box wrapped in white paper. "Spud, he gifes me a big cake,now I gif him somethings, yes!" And he handed the box over.

"What's this, another joke?" demanded the other student suspiciously.

"Do you think I play a joke?" asked Max, with a hurt look.

"All right then," said Spud, and proceeded to undo the string around the box. Then he took off the paper and opened the box.

What a shout went up! For the box was filled with potatoesplain white and sweet! There were about a quart of them, mixed.

"Oh, what a sell!" murmured Spud. "I knew you'd do something like this!" he added, grinning sheepishly.

"Better pass 'em around," suggested Tom.

"All right, have one raw!" returned Spud.

"Hi! ton't gif dem avay so kvick!" cried Max, getting excited and talking more brokenly than usual. "Besser examine dem first."

"Examine 'em?" murmured Spud. "Oh, I see!" he added, and took up one of the potatoes. "Why, it isn't a potato at all!" he exclaimed as the article came apart. "It's only a shell, and it's filled with candy!"

"Chocolate drops!" murmured Sam. "Yum! yum!"

"There are salted almonds in this one," went on Spud, opening an imitation of a sweet potato. "And here are stuffed dates, and this had raisins in itand here are soft gum drops! Say, Max, this is certainly great! How did you happen to think of it?" And Spud looked tremendously pleased.

"Oh, I know you lof potatoes," answered the GermanAmerican youth, innocently.

The candy was placed on one of the wooden plates, and the almonds and raisins on another, and then the good things were passed around.

"I'll keep these as souvenirs of the occasion," said Spud, indicating the imitation potatoes.

"How about it, Songbird, can't you rise to the occasion?" asked Dick, who had noticed that the studentpoet had been unusually quiet while eating his cake and icecream.

"I haveerjust composed a little poem in honor of Max's birthday," answered Songbird. "If you'd like me to recite"

"Sure thing!"

"Turn on the poetry spigot, Songbird, and let her flow!"

"This is not yet finished. But,but"

"Give us what you have," said Spud, and clearing his throat several times, Songbird began.

"Once more a year has rolled around
As years have rolled before
Once more we greet our loving friend
A true friend to the core!
We hope that in the future he
Will win success and fame,
And go down in our history
A noble"
Bang! came the report of a gun, and the shot was so unexpected that Songbird forgot what he was going to say, and all those at the feast sprang to their feet. Bang! came a second report.

"What does that mean?" cried Stanley. "Who is firing a gun this time of night?"

"I think I know what it means!" exclaimed Dick, leaping for the door. "Come on, if you want to save the Dartaway!" he went on, to his brothers.

CHAPTER XV

A PERILOUS FLIGHT

Without waiting to get a hat or an extra coat, Dick dashed through the long corridor and down the broad stairs of the dormitory and Tom came at his heels.

"What's the matter?" cried Spud, grabbing Sam, just as the youngest Rover boy was about to follow his brothers.

"I'll tell you when we get back," answered Sam. "Don't stop me now, please, I may be wanted."

"Want any help?" put in Songbird, who for the moment had forgotten what he was about to recite.

"I don't knowbut I guess not."

"We'll go along anyhow," came from Max, and took after Sam, while several others did the same.

In the meantime Dick and Tom had gained the lower hallway of the dormitory. The door was fastened, but the key was in the lock and they soon had the portal open and they leaped outside. Then both started in the direction of the gymnasium shed.

"See anybody?" cried Tom.

"No, it's too dark," answered Dick. "But that must have been Abner Filbury's gun."

The two reports from the shotgun had aroused many in various buildings around the campus, and windows were being raised and heads thrust out.

"What's the trouble?"

"Who fired those shots?"

"Is it a joke?"

"There go two of the Rovers!"

91

"Are they up to some trick?"

"More than likely. You can't keep Tom Rover quiet."

So the comments ran on, while Dick and Tom sped in the direction of the shed. As they came closer they received a sudden challenge from the big doorway.

"Hi! don't you dare to come back here, or I'll shoot you!" The words were uttered by Abner Filbury, who stood there, shotgun in hand and lantern by his side.

"Don't shoot!" ordered Dick. "It is I, Dick Rover! What's the trouble?"

"Oh, so it's you, Mr. Rover!" returned the janitor's son, with a sigh of relief. "I was afraid them pesky rascals was acoming back."

"What rascals?"

"The fellers as got at the airship while I was asleep. But I guess they didn't get no chance to hurt anything," went on Abner, hastily.

"Who were they?" asked Tom.

"I don't know. They had rags tied over their faces, so I couldn't see 'em."

"How many of them were there?" questioned Dick.

"Two."

"Are you sure they didn't harm anything?" went on the eldest Rover boy, as he entered the shed.

"No, I ain't sure, for when I woke up they was in the shed, right under my hammock. I got scared and I blazed away at the roof, and then they got scared, I can tell you! They jumped and let out a yell, and ran for the door, and I got down and went to the door and fired the other barrel into the air, as a warning. Then they disappeared in the darkness."

"I guess it was" began Tom, when Dick caught hold of his arm and silenced him.

"We'll take a look at the machine," said the big brother, and they went into the shed. Here they were soon joined by Sam and the others; and soon a close inspection of the biplane was in progress.

"I don't see any damage," said Dick, presently.

"Most likely they didn't have time to do any," replied Tom.

"I'm glad of it," added Sam, with a sigh of relief.

"Who would be so mean?" questioned Stanley.

"I've got my suspicions, but I won't say anything yet," answered Dick.

A proctor and several instructors had come down to the shed, and the situation had to be explained to them. All thought it mean that anybody should try to damage the flying machine.

"Perhaps it was merely a boyish trick," said Professor Blackie. "Let us hope so."

"Maybe," answered Dick. "Just the same, I am glad that I placed Filbury on guard." And then he told the young man to keep a closer watch than before, and this Abner promised to do. Then the boys went back to the dormitory, finished the feast, and went to bed.

A few days later came word that Dora and the Laning girls had arrived at Hope Seminary, and the Rovers, of course, made immediate preparations to visit them.

"We'll give 'em a surprise," said Tom, with a grin. "We'll visit 'em in the Dartaway." And this the other brothers readily agreed to do.

A message was sent to the three girls, requesting them to meet the boys at a certain hour on the campus of the seminary. Then the Rovers got the Dartaway in readiness for the trip, polishing up the engine and working parts until they shone like silver.

"If only it doesn't rain, or blow too hard," said Sam, when all was in readiness.

"Oh, we'll go anyway," cried Tom.

The boys had purchased regular aviation suits, which looked very neat and professionallike. The new engine was in place, and they had given it a good tryout and had found that it worked as well as the other and gave much more power.

"I think we could carry half a dozen folks now," said Sam, after a trial with some bags of sand. "She takes up the extra weight without an effort."

"Perhaps, but there is no use of straining the biplane, or the engine either," returned Dick.

The morning of the allimportant day came and the boys found the wind blowing steadily from the west.

"Rather breezy for a flight," was Dick's comment.

"Do you think it will rain?" queried Sam, anxiously.

"Not with the wind from that quarter, Sam. But we may get more breeze than we want."

"Oh, we won't mind the wind a bit," declared Tom, who never wanted anything to interfere with his pleasure.

The boys had their regular classes to attend during the morning, and also one recitation after lunch. But by halfpast two all were free, and after donning their aviation suits, they hurried to the shed and rolled out the Dartaway.

"Pretty breezy and no mistake," remarked Dick, as he gazed anxiously at the sky. "I don't know about this."

"Oh, don't say we can't go, Dick!" pleaded Sam.

"Maybe the breeze isn't so strong high up," came from Tom, hopefully.

"It may be stronger, Tom. We don't want to go up and get wrecked."

"Oh, the Dartaway won't get wreckednot with that powerful engine."

Dick hesitated. He did not like that strong breeze in the least. Yet he was just as anxious as his brothers to visit the seminary and meet the girls, and let them see the biplane. And there was something even more important on his mind.

"Oh, come ahead, and take a chance!" cried Tom. "We'll get through somehow!"

"Just what I say," declared Sam.

"Who is to run the machine?" asked the big brother.

"I'll run her, if you want me to," answered Tom, promptly.

"Oh, I was only thinking of the honor, Tom. I'm not afraid to try it."

"Oh, you go ahead and do it," put in Sam, who knew that his big brother's heart was set on showing Dora what he could do with the flying machine.

"We'll go up and try it," answered Dick, at last. "If she works all right, I'll head her for the seminary; otherwise I'll bring her down again;" and so it was arranged.

A number of the students had come out to see the flight and they gave a cheer as the big biplane rushed over the campus and then arose like a bird in the air. As the machine went up, Tom looked to one side and saw Dudd Flockley standing on the campus, in company with a student named Andy Yates. Both were sneering at the Rovers and their friends.

"The pair that tried to damage the machine," muttered Tom to himself. He knew that since Larkspur and Koswell had left Brill, Flockley and Yates had become quite friendly, and he also knew that Yates was a spendthrift and had a reputation far from good.

Up and up went the biplane, guided by the steady hand and keen eye of Dick. The wind rushed over the canvas planes and sang merrily through the wire stays. The engine banged away steadily, and the propellers left only a blur in the air as they kept whizzing around and around.

"How is it, Dick?" asked Sam, after a full minute had passed, and they were turning in a big circle.

"Can't tell yetpretty gusty and full of holes," was the answer, and Dick gritted his teeth tightly and took a firmer hold of the steering wheel. Then the Dartaway came around with a rush.

"Wow!" cried Tom, clutching at his seat. "Say, this is some slant!"

"Hold tight!" yelled Dick.

The warning came none too soon, for a gust of wind hit the biplane and all but made it "turn turtle," as the saying goes. But Dick was on the watch, and he sent the tips down, and soon the machine righted itself. Then they rushed away, over the woods beyond the college buildings.

"Going?" queried Sam.

"Are you game?" asked Dick, grimly.

"Sure!"

"What about it, Tom? Don't go if you don't think it is best."

"We'll try it. Dick. But if you spill us outwell, please choose a soft spot, that's all!" went on Tom, who had to have his joke, even in such a time of peril.

To take that trip, with such a wind blowing, was not a wise move, and all three of the Rovers knew it. But they wanted so much to see the girls, and show them the biplane, that they were willing to take the risk.

On and on sailed the Dartaway, now in the teeth of the breeze and then with the wind on the quarter. All of the youths clung fast constantly, for their was great danger of being pitched into space. They had straps for fastening themselves, but hated to use these, fearing that they might get in some position where a quick jump might mean safety. If they were strapped in, and the biplane fell, they might be crushed to death under the heavy engine.

Most of the trip was made in the face of the wind, which, every instant, seemed to grow stronger. The Dartaway acted like a thing of life, swooping and careening from one side to the other. Dick had to manipulate the wheel and the levers constantly, to keep anything like an even "keel."

"Can you keep to the course?" questioned Tom, after about half the distance to the seminary had been covered.

"I don't knowit depends on the wind," Dick replied. "I may go around to the westwardit seems to be better sailing that way."

In the end they had to make a wide detour, and Dick was wondering how he was going to turn in the direction of Hope Seminary, when the wind suddenly died down. This was his chance, and on the instant he headed directly for the seminary.

"There it is!" cried Sam, presently. "I see the buildings!"

"There is the campus!" added Tom, a minute later. "And there are the girls, waving banners at us!"

"I see them!" answered Dick, and then he shut off the engine, and silently and with the grace of a big, white swan, the Dartaway volplaned to the earth.

CHAPTER XVI

DICK AND DORA

"Oh, Dick, how lovely!"

"Weren't you afraid, Sam?"

"What a big flying machine, Tom!"

Such were the exclamations from Dora, Grace and Nellie, as all rushed forward to where the boys were alighting from the Dartaway. Soon they were shaking hands all around, and soon other girl students were coming up, to learn what the arrival of the flying machine meant.

"Well, we certainly had a great trip," said Dick.

"The wind was pretty strong," put in Sam.

"Strongest wind you ever saw!" declared Tom, stoutly. "Turned us over about 'steen times and rolled us into a regular ball."

"Oh, Tom, what an idea!" exclaimed Nellie, and began to laugh. "But weren't you afraid?" she went on anxiously.

"What, me? Never! But Sam was so afraid he shook off his shoes, and one of 'em dropped right on a cow, and"

"Tom Rover!" burst out Grace. "What a storyteller you are!"

"Well, Grace, if you don't believe it, go and ask that cow," went on the funloving Rover, soberly. "It's lucky Sam has elastics on the shoesto pull 'em back by. If he hadn't had" Tom did not finish but shook his head mournfully.

"I am so glad you got here safely, Dick," said Dora, in a low voice. "But oh, do you think it is quite safe?" she went on, anxiously. "II don't want you to get hurt!"

"I guess it is safe enough, Dora," he replied, not wishing to alarm her. "It's like an autoyou've got to get used to it."

"I don't think I'd ever get used to a flying machine."

"Maybe you would. Some day I'll take you up and you can see how you like it." But Dora shook her head at this.

The boys had hoped to have a quiet time with the three girls, but this was not to be just then. The students of the seminary gathered around, and the lads were kept busy explaining about the biplane, and how the engine and the steering gear worked. Then, to show that they could run the Dartaway as well as Dick, Tom took the machine up and Sam followed him, each making several circles around the campus.

"Any girls want to go up?" questioned Tom. "Now don't please all speak at once." There was a general giggle, but nobody accepted the invitation. Then the Rovers turned to those they had come to visit, and, taking the hint, the other girl students sauntered away.

"Wouldn't you like some refreshments?" asked Dora. "We might get some hot coffee and some cake."

"No, we'll have to get back before dark," answered Dick. "So we'll just stay and talk awhile. Any special news from home?"

"No. Mamma is going away for her health, and Mrs. Laning is going with her."

"I hope they go where old Crabtree and Sobber can't find them."

"That is what they are going to try to do, Dick. Oh, dear, I wish those people would never come near us again!"

"They are up near our home now," answered the eldest Rover boy, and told about the old mill.

"Whatever are they up to now, do you think, Dick?"

"I can't imagine. We are all awaiting developments."

"Your folks ought to be on guard."

"They are on guardand dad has hired a detective to keep his eye on Crabtree and Sobber."

"What about your father, Dick? You wrote that he was worried over some business matter."

"He is, and Uncle Randolph is worried, too, Dora. It's some business you wouldn't understandsomething about some western investment. You see dad and uncle are getting old and they can't watch things as they used toand Uncle Randolph is all wrapped up in scientific farming, just as he always was. I sometimes think it's time I took hold of business matters and helped them."

"Then you'd have to leave Brill, wouldn't you?"

"Yes; but I'd not mind thatI have a pretty good education even now, and I could study in my spare moments. I could take a short course, instead of one of the long ones. And then, Dora, that would help out another way," went on Dick in a lower voice, and looking over his shoulder to make sure that the others were not listening. But the others had walked off to the rear of the big biplane.

"Another way? How?" And Dora looked at him wonderingly.

"Oh, you know well enough."

"No, I don't," she replied; but two bright spots began to show in her pretty cheeks, making her prettier than ever.

"Well, I made up my mind that as soon as I left college I was going to get married," Dick went on, looking her full in the eyes.

"Oh, Dick!" And now she cast her eyes on the ground.

"Sure. Don't you think it's a good idea?" he went on, and he caught her hand and held it.

"Oh, II" She blushed more than ever and could not go on.

"I know we are not so very old, Dora, but, on the other hand, we are not so very young either, and I think your mother would approve, and I am sure my father wouldn't object. I know he thinks you are just the finest girl in the whole world,he said so."

"Well, mamma likes you, too, Dick,she's told me that many times."

"Then I'm sure she won't object. And, besides, when I'm her soninlaw I'll be able to do a good deal more than I can nowabout helping her with her financial affairs, and all that, you know."

"Yes, I know that, too."

"And so I think we ought to get married. But, of course, if you object, Dora"

"Did I object?" And she smiled just a littlea smile that set his heart bounding.

"Then you'll consent?" he asked eagerly. "Will you? Say yes, won't you?" And now he had hold of both of her hands and was looking her full in the eyes. "I want you so much, Dora,I've wanted you ever since I first met youon that little steamboat, on the way to Putnam Hall."

"Oh, Dick, what an idea! Why, you hardly knew me then!"

"Never mind, I knew you well enough."

"What a long time ago that was," murmured the girl. She was still gazing fully into his eyes.

"Yes, it was a long time ago, and yet, somehow, it seems an awfully short time, too. But, Dora, you haven't said yes yet. Won't you please say yes?" he pleaded, in a lower voice, as Tom and the others started to rejoin them.

"Yes," she murmured, her face becoming a rosy red. "Yes. Any time you say, Dick, if mamma is willing."

"You dear, dear girl!" he cried softly. "Oh, I just wish I had you all to myself for a moment!" And he gave her a look that spoke volumes.

"Well, we've got to get back, that is all there is to it," came from Sam loudly. He could not help but notice how confidential Dick and Dora were becoming.

"I'd like to stay, but we've got to make the trip before it gets too dark," added Tom.

"Just as you say," answered Dick, although he did not, just then, see how he was going to tear himself away.

But the boys did not leave for a good quarter of an hour, and during that time, Dick and Dora somehow managed to walk to the end of the campus, where there were big clumps of rose bushes and lilac shrubbery. Once in the shadow of these Dick pulled something from a pocket and held it out to Dora.

"If we are going to be regularly engaged, you must have this," he said.

"Oh, Dick, a diamond ring!" she cried, as the glint of the jewel caught her eyes.

"Hold out your hand, dear," he said, and when she held it out he placed the ring on her finger. Then he took her in his arms.

"Mine, Dora, mine, always and forever mine!"

"Always, and forever, Dick!" she answered. And then they kissed each other.

When they rejoined the others each felt as if walking on air.

"But the ringthey'll be sure to see it, Dick!" whispered Dora.

"If they don't I shall be disappointed," he answered.

It was Grace who espied the glittering circlet first and she uttered a slight shriek. Then she pointed it out to her sister.

"A diamond ringan engagement ring!" she cried.

"Oh, how lovely!" exclaimed Nellie.

"Ladies and gentlemen, the future Mrs. Dick Rover!" said Dick, just a bit awkwardly, while Dora blushed the color of a peony.

"Oh, Dora!" cried Grace and Nellie, in chorus, and then each kissed her.

"I thought I smelt a mouse," murmured Sam.

"Hail to the bride!" cried Tom. "Say, Dick, isn't it proper to salute your future sisterinlaw?" he went on, with a broad grin.

"I don't knowbetter ask her," replied Dick, goodnaturedly, and then Tom kissed Dora, and Sam did the same thing. After that Tom declared he ought to kiss the "bridetobe's cousins," and started in, and Sam followed.

"Here, you kids break away!" cried Dick finally. "I thought you said we had to get back before dark."

"'Kids' indeed!" snorted Tom. "My, how old we've gotten since we're engaged!" And then he grinned more than ever. "But never mind," he went on to Nellie, in a whisper. "Just you wait and see the diamond ring I get you one of these days." And this remark made Nellie blush as deeply as had Dora. Sam said something, too, to Grace about a ring, at which she laughed merrily and slapped his face. But when the boys were in the biplane and ready to sail away, and he held up a finger with a ring on it and looked at her questioninglyand longinglyshe gave a quick little nod of her curly head.

"OH, DICK, A DIAMOND RING!" SHE CRIED
"All ready?" asked Dick, at last.

"All ready!" replied his brothers.

"Then start her up!" cried the oldest Rover boy, and the others gave a turn to the propellers. Bang! bang! bang! went the engine, and Sam and Tom rushed to their seats.

"Come again soon!" cried the girls.

"Just as soon as we can!" was the answer.

"Be careful!" pleaded Dora. "Please, please be careful!"

"We'll look outdon't worry," answered Dick. He had to shout, to make himself heard above the noise of the motor. Then came the usual whizz and rush, and a few seconds later the Rover boys were once more in the air and bound for Brill.

Dick would have been pleased could he have allowed his mind to linger on the conversation he had had with Dora, but he soon found this out of the question. The wind had come up again, and was now blowing as strongly as ever, and he had all he could do to manage the Dartaway. Soon the big biplane commenced to pitch and toss like a small boat on the bosom of an angry ocean.

"Say, this is getting something fierce!" was Sam's comment, after a particularly thrilling dip. "I thought we were going right down that time."

"You hold tight!" yelled Dick. "Don't let go for an instant."

"I'm as tight as glue," was the reply.

"Hadn't you better go up a bit, Dick?" came from Tom.

"Just what I thought of doing," was the answer.

The rudders were shifted, and swiftly the biplane mounted through space. It was now growing dark, and presently the panorama that had been below them, vanished from view.

"Huh! This won't do!" cried Dick. "I can't see how to steer."

"Steer by the wind for awhile," suggested Sam.

A minute later came a fierce gust of wind, followed by a second and then a third. Around spun the biplane and then tilted up as if about to go over. Then came an unexpected ripping and tearing sound.

"It's the left planeit's torn loose!" yelled Sam. "Let her down, Dick, before it is too late! If you don't, we'll drop to our death!"

CHAPTER XVII

CAUGHT IN A HAILSTORM

All of the Rover boys realized their extreme peril, yet for the moment they were powerless to do anything to help themselves. Dick put out his hand to stop the engine of the biplane, then concluded that it might be more advantageous to keep the propellers moving.

Around and around spun the flying machine, tossed like a chip on an angry ocean. All grew dark about the three boys and each gave himself up for lost. It was useless to attempt to steer, so Dick held the craft as she was, so far as the wheel was concerned.

Then came a sudden, sickening drop and a tilting to one side. Sam let out a wild yell, but what he said was drowned out in the roaring of the wind and the noise of the engine. Then, of a sudden, the Dartaway dove forward and the gust of air was left behind. They came into a "hole," as it is termed by aviators, and again they sank. But now Dick was gaining control once more and he tilted the front rudder and up they went for a hundred feet, but in something of a circle, because of the broken plane.

"Can't you land?" gasped Tom. "We can'tcan'tstandthis!"

"I'll do what I can," replied Dick, between his set teeth. He knew that their very lives depended on how he handled the biplane.

Slowly and with great caution Dick allowed the Dartaway to get closer to the earth. Each of the boys strained his eyes, to catch sight of what might be below. Then came another gust, and this was followed by a strange rattling on the biplane. Small, white objects were bouncing in all directions.

"It's hail!" cried Sam. "We've struck a hail squall!"

He was right, and the hail continued to come down all around them, driven by a sweeping wind that carried the Dartaway hither and thither. But it was one of those sudden squalls that do not last long, and soon they were sailing in the clear air again, and now within view of the ground below.

"There is a fine fieldto the right," cried Tom.

105

Dick nodded and, not without an effort, brought the biplane around. Then he shut off the motor, and they slid to earth quicker than they had anticipated. The Dartaway struck the ground and bounced up and down several times on its rubbertired wheels and then came to a standstill in the midst of some brushwood. Poor Sam was thrown out heels over head into the bushes.

"Are you hurt?" sang out Dick, anxiously. It was so dark he could not see what had become of his youngest brother.

"II guess not!" came back from Sam, and he started to scramble out of the bushes. "Say, that was some sail, wasn't it?" he continued.

"No more like that for me!" returned Tom, panting like a race horse. "Are you O. K., Dick?"

"Yes, although that bumping shook me up. But come, fasten the Dartaway down before the wind comes up again and blows it to kingdom come!"

This warning was necessary for the wind was still fitful and there was no telling how strong it might become. All sprang forward to do what they could to save the biplane from destruction.

"If there was a barn handy we might use that," said Sam.

They looked around, but the only building nearby was a small cottage, evidently one used by a farmer's hired hands.

"Run her around between the bushes," directed Dick. "They will protect her a little, for the bushes are quite high."

They found a spot between the undergrowth and into it forced the biplane, until the air craft was completely surrounded. The bushes broke the force of the wind and the lads had little difficulty in tying the machine fast with the ropes they always carried. It was hailing again, although not so heavily as before. The wind was gradually going down, but the sky was as dark and threatening as ever.

"I think it will turn into rain before very long," said Dick, after a look around. "Too bad it couldn't have held off half an hour longer. Then we'd have been safe at Brill."

"I'm thankful we got down safely, Dick," said Sam.

"Oh, so am I!"

"It was a narrow escape," was Tom's comment. "Great hambones! Who would have thought we'd run into such weather as this!"

"Oh, hailstorms like this are not uncommon, even in midsummer," answered Dick. "Don't you remember the one that came and cut down our corn some years ago?"

"Yes, and broke all the glass in the hothouse," added Sam. "Say, is the machine hurt much?" he went on.

"We'll have to make an examination."

They looked the biplane over as best they could in the semidarkness. One of the bamboo poles had been split and two of the canvas stretches were slit from end to end.

"Not as bad as it might be," said Dick. "We can easily mend the canvas. But I guess we had better get a new pole in place of that one. I'd not care to trust it, even if it were wired."

"Perhaps we can wire it good enough to get back to Brill with," returned Tom. "We can't stay here."

"I've had enough sailing for today!" cried Sam. "Let us walk back, or get a carriage, and leave the biplane here until some fine day when there is no wind."

"Yes, we can't use her any more today," said Dick. "Let us cover the engine and walk to that cottage and find out just where we are, and how we can get to Brill."

Having arranged everything as well as the means at hand permitted, the three Rover boys left the vicinity of the brushwood and walked over to where the small cottage was located. The ground was covered with hailstones and Tom could not resist the temptation to gather up a handful and pelt his brothers.

"Stop it!" cried Sam, and then, as Tom would not stop, he rushed in with some of the hailstones in his hand and allowed them to slide down inside of Tom's collar.

"Wow!" roared the funloving Rover. "Let up, Sam! That feels as if I'd hit the North Pole!"

"Then you let up," answered Sam, firmly; and after that Tom let the hailstones alone.

As they neared the cottage they saw that a lantern was lit and set on a table in the centre of the living room. Around the table sat three persons, two young fellows and an older man, evidently a farmer. The three were smoking and playing cards, and on the table lay some bankbills.

"Why, look at this!" cried Dick, in astonishment. Then he added quickly: "Get out of sight, don't show yourselves!" And he caught each of his brothers by the arm and led the pair to the rear of the building.

"What's up, Dick?" asked Sam. "Who were they?"

"Didn't you recognize those young fellows?"

"I did!" cried Tom, in a low voice. "They were Jerry Koswell and Bart Larkspur!"

"Koswell and Larkspur!" exclaimed Sam. "Are you sure?"

"Tom is right," replied Dick.

"Who was the third fellow?"

"I don't know. He looked like a farmer to me."

"Did you see the money on the table?" broke out Tom. "They must have been gambling!"

"It looked that way to me, Tom."

"If they were, all I've got to say, that third fellow better look out for Koswell and Larkspur," continued Tom. "They are sharpers at cards, so Dudd Flockley once told me. He said they got him to put up his money a number of times and each time they won. He was inclined to think they didn't play fairly."

"Well, knowing them as we do, I'd say they wouldn't be above cheating," said Sam. "But what in the world can they be doing in this outoftheway place?"

"That remains to be found out," replied his big brother. "Maybe they were on the road and ran here for shelter from the hailstorm."

"I'm not afraid of them, Dick," said Tom.

"Neither am I, Tom, you know that."

"Then what's the use of keeping out of sight? I'd rather go in there and give them a thrashing, like the one we gave them on that island."

"Don't forget we have the Dartaway here and they might take pleasure in ruining the craft or running off with her. Besides, I'd like to watch them a bit and find out a little about their plans. Remember, they want to play us some dirty trick."

"There they go!" burst out Sam, at that instant, and motioned to the front of the cottage. All looked in the direction he pointed out, to see Koswell and Larkspur hurrying down a lane that led to a road running between the trees.

"You come back here! That wasn't fair!" shouted the farm hand who had been playing cards with them. "Come back!" And he rushed to the front door of the cottage and waved his arm wildly.

"It was fair!" shouted back Jerry Koswell.

"Sure it was fair!" added Bart Larkspur. "We'd come back, only we are in a hurry."

"You cheated me!" stormed the farm hand and shook his fist at the pair. But they paid no further attention, and soon the darkness and a bend of the road hid them from view.

The Rover boys waited a few seconds and then knocked on the back door of the cottage. The farm hand, a fellow named Dan Murdock, stamped over to the door and threw it open.

"What do you want?" he asked surlily. The loss of his money had made him illtempered.

"Why, hello, Murdock!" cried Sam. "I didn't know you lived here."

"Oh, so it's you, Rover," answered the farm hand. He remembered that he had once given Sam a ride and had been well paid for it. "Caught in the hailstorm?" he went on, a bit more pleasantly.

"Yes. These are my brothers," added Sam. "We were out and we got lost. Can you tell us the best road to the college?"

"Of course. Walk through the woods back there. Then take the road to the left and at the cross roads turn to the right. You'll see the signs, so you can't go wrong."

"And how far is it?"

"About two miles. You can take the road yonder, too, but that's about a mile longer."

"Do you live here?" asked Dick, curiously.

"I sleep hereme and two other hands. We get our meals up to Mr. Dawson's housethe man we work for."

"Oh, then this is the Dawson farm?" Dick remembered that Mr. Dawson supplied butter and eggs to the college.

"Yes, sir."

"I'm glad to know that, for we need some help. We were out in our flying machine and had to come down over there. We'll want somebody to look after the machine until we can fix it up and take it away. Of course we'll pay for what's done," he added.

"Oh, I heard tell of that flying machine!" exclaimed the farm hand. "You sailed over this farm a couple of hours ago."

He was much interested and wanted to know all about the trip, and about the machine. He said Mr. Dawson was away, but that the Dartaway could be wheeled up into one of the big barns and left there until repaired. Then he agreed to get out a twoseated carriage and drive the boys over to Brill. Inside of half an hour the biplane was safely housed, and the whole party was on the way to the college.

Dick had warned Sam and Tom to remain silent concerning Koswell and Larkspur, and it was not until they were almost to Brill that he mentioned the fact that they had seen the pair running away from the cottage.

"Seen 'em, did you?" cried Dan Murdock. "Say, them fellers are swindlers, they are! They came in to git out of the hail and then they started to play cards, just to while away the time, so they said. They asked me to play, and as I couldn't work just then, I consented, and then they got me to put up some money,just to make it interestin', they said. They let me win a little at first, and then they got me to put up more and more, and then they cheated me and wiped me out!"

"And how much did they get from you?" asked Dick.

"They got nearly all my savingseighty dollars!" answered Dan Murdock, grimly.

110

CHAPTER XVIII

TOM AND HIS FUN

"Got eighty dollars from you!" murmured Dick. "That's too bad!"

"It would be bad enough if I lost it fairly," answered the farm hand. "But I am sure they swindled me."

"Well, you ought not to gamble," put in Sam, who had listened to the talk with interest.

"I suppose that's true," mumbled Dan Murdock. "But they said I might win a pile. Oh, I was a big foolI know it now, even if I didn't know it then. I wish I had stopped 'em from leaving."

"Why didn't you?"

"They went so sudden likeafter they had my money. One of 'em took out his watch and said they'd miss the train, and away they started before you could say Jack Robinson! But there ain't no train this time o' day."

"It was a trick to get away," said Tom.

"SureI know that, now! Oh, if only I had my hands on 'em. Say, they don't belong at Brill, do they?" went on the farm hand eagerly.

"No, although they used to go there," answered Dick.

"Then you saw 'em?"

"Yes, we saw them running away."

"What are their names?" and when Dick had mentioned them Dan Murdock shook his head slowly.

"I've heard of 'em before," he said. "They used to hang around at the tavern. I was a big fool, no two ways about it! I guess they'll keep out of my sight after this."

"More than likely," answered Dick.

When the boys arrived at the college they found an anxious crowd looking for them and the biplane. Songbird and Stanley and several others rushed to the carriage to greet them.

"Were you wrecked?"

"Did you get a bad tumble?"

"Where did you come down?"

So the questions ran on and the boys had to answer as best they could. Everybody seemed to be glad to learn that they had escaped from the fury of the sudden hailstormthat is, everybody but Dudd Flockley and his new crony, Andy Yates.

"Just like the Rovers' luck," muttered Flockley, sourly. "They'd escape where everybody else would be smashed up."

"Oh, they'll get a smash, if you give 'em time enough," answered Andy Yates, heartlessly. He was a student who courted attention and it galled him to see the Rovers the center of attraction.

As soon as Dick, Tom and Sam could get time to do so, they sent a message to Hope Seminary, informing the girls that they had gotten back to Brill in safety. This relieved much anxiety, for with the sudden coming of the wind and hail the girls had feared that the youths might be killed.

After such a strenuous adventure, the Rover boys were content to take it easy for some time. They sent to the city for a man to come and repair the Dartaway and then settled down to their studies. Then, after the biplane had been repaired, they went after the machine and brought it back to Brill, and it was placed in the gymnasium shed, with Abner Filbury to guard it, as before.

"Don't you want to go up, Songbird?" asked Tom, one afternoon, after college hours.

"IerI don't think so," answered the studentpoet, gravely.

"Rather make up verses about flying than fly, eh?"

"IerI think so, Tom."

"What have you made up about airships, anything really fine, Songbird?"

"Well, I've written a few little verses, Tom. Would you like to hear them?"

"Sure!" cried the funloving Rover, and then Songbird commenced to recite:

"I spread my wings on the balmy air,
And float and float I know not where.
I rise, I fall, I fall, I rise,
For I am monarch of the skies!"
"Bang up, Songbird! Couldn't be better!" cried Tom. "Give us another dip, like the small boy said of the icecream." And the wouldbe poet continued:

"I rush along when skies are blue,
And when it hails I sail right through!
I feel"
"Hold on, Songbird! You've got to change that line. We didn't sail right through when it hailedwe came down just as quickly as we could."

"Oh, that's only a figure of speech," answered the wouldbe poet loftily, and then he continued:

"I feel I can sail anywhere,
For I am monarch of the air!"
"Good for you!" put in Sam, who was present. "For A, No. , firstgrade poetry apply to Songbird every time."

"There are sixteen verses in all," went on the poet, eagerly. "The next one begins"

"Sorry, there goes the supper bell!" interrupted Tom. "Come on, we've got to eat, even if we miss the finest poem in the universe."

"IerI didn't hear any bell," answered Songbird.

"You didn't?" cried Tom, innocently. "Well! well! Come on in and see anyway!" And he dragged the wouldbe poet along and forced him into a crowd of students. "Guess I was mistaken," he said soberly. "Too bad!" And off he, ran, and Sam ran after him.

"Well, it wasn't half bad," said the youngest Rover.

"That's true, Sam," returned Tom, and then he added with a sudden broad grin: "But how about an egg that was only half badwould you want to eat it? Some day Songbird may write real poetrybut not yet."

It was now ideal football weather and the football elevens, the regular and the scrub, were out daily for practice. Dick and Tom had been asked to play but both had declined, for they wished to pay attention to their studies, and the biplane took up all their spare time. Sam played a little on the scrub, but soon gave it up.

During those days Dick was more serious than usual, and neither Tom nor Sam bothered their elder brother. They knew he was thinking of his engagement to Dora, and also worrying over the business affairs of their father and their Uncle Randolph.

One day Tom and Sam took a short trip in the biplane and persuaded Stanley to go with them, and the next day they took out Spud. But nobody else of their chums cared to go.

"A new arrival tomorrow!" cried Sam, one evening. "Just from a trip to Paris, too."

"Is it William Philander Tubbs?" queried Tom, looking up from the theme he was writing.

"You've struck it, Tom. Since you wrote to him about the socks he has been over to Paris. But he gets back to the grind tomorrowcomes in on the fourthirty train."

"Say, let us get up a reception in William's honor!" cried the funloving Rover; and as soon as the theme was finished he began to arrange his plans.

The next afternoon the Rovers and a crowd of their chums took one of the college carryalls and drove over to Ashton station to witness the sport. Tom had been to town early in the morning and had arranged matters with eight colored waiters from the hotel, and also with a local liveryman.

As the train came in the boys and a number of others were on the watch for Tubbs. As soon as they saw the dudish student alight, dresssuit case in hand, the Rovers rushed up to him.

"How are you, Sir William!" cried Dick, taking the dude's hand gravely.

"Let me congratulate you, Lord Tubbs!" cried Sam, bowing low.

"Your Highness will find his carriage this way," put in Tom, taking the dresssuit case and flinging it to one of the colored men.

"Whyerweally, don't you know, what doeserthis mean?" stammered poor William Philander, gazing around in astonishment.

And well might he be astonished, for there, before him, in a wideopen double row, stood the eight colored men, all dressed in black, with broad red sashes over their breasts and cockades of red paper in their hats. On the platform between the colored men was a bright red stair carpet, and this carpet led directly to where a carriage was in waiting. The carriage had four white horses, all decorated in red ribbons, and on the seat sat a driver, also decorated in red.

"Such an honor to have your Lordship condescend to come to Brill," went on Tom, with a low bow.

"What did the Queen say when she decorated you?" asked Dick.

"It was a grand thing for the King to honor you so highly," put in Sam.

"I certainly envy you," came from Songbird, who was in the secret.

"Hope there is a good salary attached to the office," was Stanley's comment.

"I've heard it vas fife thousand pounds by the year!" vouchsafed Max.

"How the girls will fall in love with you when they hear of this," sighed Spud.

"This way, your Excellency!" cried Tom, and led poor, bewildered Tubbs to the carriage.

"Thomas, my dear fellow, whaterwhat does it mean?" gasped the dudish student, his eyes opening wider and wider.

"Oh, you can't fool us, Tubblets," whispered the funloving Rover. "You were going to keep it a secret, but we read all about it in the London paper one of the fellows sent over."

"Read aboutahwhat, please?"

"Why, how the king and queen knighted you, and all that, Philliam Whilander."

"William Philander, please, Thomas. Buterthis is a mistake"

"No, no, Tubby, my boy, no mistake at all, I assure you. This is in your honor solely. The college faculty did itthey couldn't do less, to one so decorated, or knighted,which is it, please? It's the grandest thing that ever happened to Brill."

"But don't you know, IerI haven't beenerknighted, or anything else. I wasn't in England, I went to Paris, and"

"Now, now, my dear boy, don't try that game," said Tom, reproachfully. "We all know perfectly well that you were knighted and that you are now Sir Tubbs, P. X. C., and all that. We salute you!" And then Tom took off his hat. "Three cheers for Sir Tubbs!" he called loudly.

The cheers were given with a will, and a tiger added. Poor Tubbs was almost stricken dumb, and commenced to mop the perspiration from his forehead.

"Don't crowd so close!" cried Tom, warningly. "His Lordship must have air! He isn't used to so much excitement! Stand back! Now then, into the carriage, if you please!" And into the turnout went poor Tubbs, and the next instant his hat was snatched from his head and a tall, white beaver was placed in its stead. Then several medals of tin and brass were pinned to his coat, and the crowd set up a riotous cheering.

"Hurrah for Sir Tubbs!"

"My, what an honor for Brill!"

"Nothing like having a real nobleman for a student!"

"Away we go! Pile in, boys!" cried Tom, and then there was a crack of a whip, and off the strange turnout started, with poor Tubbs on the seat looking more bewildered than ever, and followed by the great carryall with the yelling and singing students who had come to greet him.

116

CHAPTER XIX

STARTLING NEWS FROM HOME

"Here the conquering hero comes!"

"Say, but he looks like a real Lord, doesn't he?"

"Don't forget to bow to all the people you pass, Sir Tubbs!"

So the cries rang on, as the carriage and the carryall rolled away from the Ashton depot.

"Say, look here, what does this mean?" stammered the dudish student. "I tell you I'm no lord, or knight, or anything like that! I was over to Paris, not London, don't you know. Weally, this iservery embarrassing!" he pleaded, wildly.

"Stand up and make a speech, when you get to the campus, Willie boy!" sang out Tom. "Give 'em something grand on high finance, or railroad building, or cooking beans, or something like that."

"Why, Tom, weally, don't you know, I know nothing oferrailroads, orerbeans. Please stop the carriage, I wish to get out. This iserawful, don't you know!" fairly panted the dude. He had stood up, but now the carriage gave a jolt and down he sat very suddenly.

On through the town and straight for the college drove the two turnouts, the students yelling themselves hoarse. Many at Brill had been let into the secret, and when the grounds were reached a big crowd was congregated, to take part in the sport.

"Here they are!"

"Hurrah for Lord Tubbs!"

"How are you, Duke William Philander!"

"Do you wear the order of the Red Garter?"

"No, it's the Blue Suspender he was decorated with."

"Speech! speech!" came the cry from every side.

Then the carriage came to a halt and was immediately surrounded by a howling mob. A few had flowers that they threw at William Philander, while others had supplied themselves with stalks of celery, carrot and beet tops, and similar things, which they sent forward with force and directness.

"Here's a bouquet for you!"

"My kindest regards, Tubbs!"

"Oh, isn't it grand to be a real, live Emperor!"

"Hi, let up, will you!" fairly shrieked poor Tubbs, as the things hit him in the head and shoulders, "Let up, I tell you! Oh, what a joke! Let me get out of the carriage! I can't make a speech! Stop throwing at me! Oh, my eye!" he added, as a beet top caught him in the left optic. Then, watching his chance, he leaped from the carriage, dove like a madman through the crowd, and rushed for one of the dormitories, quickly disappearing from view.

"Good bye, my boy, good bye!" sang out several. And then Tom sent the dresssuit case after him; and the fun came to an end.

"Poor William Philander, he won't forget that in a hurry!" was Dick's comment. "Just the same, I am afraid the sport got a little too rough at the end."

"Maybe it did," answered Tom. "If you want it, I'll speak to Tubbs and apologize."

"I see that apology in a gold frame right now!" declared Sam, with a laugh. "Tom, let him alone and he'll be all right."

All of the boys wondered how Tubbs would act when he showed himself. Much to their amazement he called Tom to one side that evening and shook hands cordially.

"It was all a mistakethis report that I haderbeen knighted, don't you know," he lisped. "But it was very nice to get up such a reception in my honor, Thomas, really it wasalthough it got a bit rough towards the end. But I know it was meant well, and I thank you, honestly I do." And the dudish student shook Tom's hand again.

And then, for once in his life, Tom Rover didn't know what to say. As he afterwards admitted, he was completely "stumped." Poor, innocent Tubbs had really thought it an honor! To Tom that was "the limit."

118

"I'll never really know that chap," he said to his brothers. "His head must be filled with sawdust and punk."

"Well, let him drop now," advised Dick. "Quit your fooling, Tom, and get at your studies. You know what I told you. We may have to leave Brill before we anticipated. And we want to get all the learning we can."

"Have you heard anything more from dad?" demanded the funloving Rover quickly.

"Yes, a letter came this evening. That business affair is in a worse twist than ever. But dad hopes he can straighten it out. But he writes that he isn't feeling as well as he was. If he gets sick, we'll have to jump inor at least I willand take his place."

"We'll all jump in," was Sam's comment. "I'd like to do something in a business way."

"Did dad give any particulars?" asked Tom.

"None but what we already know. He felt too ill to write much."

"Has he heard anything more of Crabtree or Sobber?"

"Nothing."

During the following week there was some excitement at Brill because of a football game between that college and another institution of learning. It was a gala occasion, and the Rover boys hired a threeseated carriage and brought Dora, Nellie and Grace to the game. Brill won the contest, and a great jubilee lasting far into the night followed. The Rovers and the three girls had a little feast of their own at the Ashton hotel, and on the way back to Hope the young people sang songs, and had a good time generally. Perhaps some very sentimental things were saidespecially between Dick and Dorabut if so, who can blame them? The placing of that engagement ring on Dora's finger by Dick had made them both exceedingly happy.

During those days the boys took several short trips in the Dartaway, once landing in the field on the Dawson farm. They sought out Dan Murdock and asked him if he had seen anything more of Koswell and Larkspur.

"Yes, I see 'em last week, but they got out of sight in the woods, and I couldn't find 'em," answered the farm hand.

"Around here?" asked Dick.

"No, that was on the edge of the big woods back of Hope Seminary. I was driving along, with some crates of eggs for the girls' college, when I see 'em, sitting on a fallen tree, smoking cigarettes. I stopped my hosses and spoke to 'em, and then they up and run into the woods as fast as they could go! I looked for 'em, but I couldn't git on their track nohow."

"What can they be doing up around Hope?" murmured Sam.

"Maybe they are sweet on some of the girls," returned Tom. "I know they used to go up there, when they attended Brill."

"I hope, if they visit Hope, they don't speak to Dora and the others," said Dick, as his face clouded.

"Maybe we better warn the girls," said Sam.

"No, don't do that," said Tom. "You'd only scare them. They know Koswell and Larkspur well enough. Don't say anything." And so the matter was dropped.

Two days later came a special delivery letter from home that filled the three boys with intense interest.

"Josiah Crabtree and Tad Sobber have at last shown their hand," wrote Mr. Anderson Rover. "They have sent an unsigned communication to me demanding fifty thousand dollars. They give me just two weeks in which to get the money together in cash and place it at a certain spot along the road between our home and Oak Run. If the money is not forthcoming they promise to blow up every building on the farm. The communication says, 'You can pay half of this and get the other half from your lady friends.' Which means, of course, the Stanhopes and Lanings."

"Of all the cowardly things!" cried Tom, after listening to the above. "Why, it's a regular sort of Black Hand communication!"

"So it is," added Sam. "What else does dad say," he went on, and Dick continued the reading of the letter:

"At first I was inclined to treat the communication lightly and laugh at it, but then came another lettera mere scrawl, stating they would give me a taste of what to expect that night. I told the detective of this and he came to the house and remained all night with us. About three o'clock in the morning there was an explosion outside, and when we dressed and ran out we found one of the chicken houses blown to flinders by dynamite or some other explosive. About one hundred chickens were destroyed."

"Just listen to that!" gasped Tom. "Oh, the rascals!"

"And Uncle Randolph's prize stock chickens!" murmured Sam. "That must have made his heart ache!"

"I'll wager Aunt Martha was scared to death," added Tom. And Dick read on:

"Of course there was great excitement, and four of us, the detective, Ness, Pop, and myself, went after the rascals, leaving your Uncle Randolph to look after your aunt and the cook, both of whom were very much frightened. We hunted around until daylight, but without success. Then we went to the old mill in the auto, but the place was deserted. After that I notified the local authorities, and I have hired ten watchmen to guard the farm and every building on it. I have also sent for two more detectives, and I am hoping that, sooner or later, they will be able to trace the scoundrels and run them down."

"Does he say how he is feeling?" questioned Sam, as his brother paused in the reading of the letter.

"Yes, he says he is about the same, but that Uncle Randolph is very much upset over the loss of his chickens and wants to know if they hadn't better pay the money demanded."

"Oh, I hope they don't pay a cent!" cried Tom.

"So do I," added Sam. "But I don't want to see them blown up either," he continued, seriously.

"None of us want that," said Dick. "But I'd not give them a centI'd be blown up a dozen times before I'd do it!" he continued, firmly.

"Do they want us home?" asked Tom.

"No, dad says it will do no good for us to come home. He says he will write or telegraph if anything new develops. He thinks, with the extra watchmen on guard, and the detectives at work, Crabtree and Sobber will get scared and leave them alone."

"I hope they do," said Sam. He heaved a deep sigh. "Gracious! it seems to me that no sooner are we out of one trouble than we get into another!"

"That is true."

"It's too badto have this piled on poor dad when he's so worried about that business affair."

"Well, you know the old saying, 'troubles never come singly,'" answered the older brother.

After that the three boys watched the mails anxiously for over a week. Then came another letter from their father, in which he stated that nothing new had developed. Then came another waituntil the day after that set by Crabtree and Sobber for the delivery of the fifty thousand dollars,when Dick got a telegram, as follows:

"All quiet. Received another letter, to which I have paid no attention. Feel almost sure the rascals have left this part of the country. All fairly well."

"Well, that's some comfort," was Tom's comment. "I hope they have gone away, and that we never see or hear of them again."

"Don't comfort yourself that way, Tom," answered Dick. "They are bound to show their hand again, sooner or later. We won't be safe from them until they are in jail."

CHAPTER XX

GRACE'S REVELATION

One clear afternoon the three Rover boys decided to take a run up to Hope Seminary in the Dartaway. There was very little wind and, although it was growing colder, they knew they could easily bundle up in their aviation coats and boots. Sam and Tom had been trying out the biplane, and they pronounced everything in perfect order for a flight.

"Dick, let me run the machine over," said Sam, and the big brother agreed, for Tom had been at the wheel on a previous occasion.

The boys had no classes to attend after lunch and so got away by two o'clock.

"I trust we can see the girls," said Dick, as they started up the engine of the flying machine.

"Oh, they'll be at liberty after hours," answered Tom. "They always are."

Previous to leaving, the boys had filled the oil feed and the gasoline tank, so they were prepared for quite a trip.

"Maybe we can get the girls to go up, for just a little sail, you know," said Sam. "I am sure the Dartaway could carry them, on a pinch."

"Where would they sit, in our laps?" asked Tom, with a grin.

"No, they could sit in the seats and we could sit back of them, like on a bobsled," answered the youngest Rover.

"I don't think they'll care to go up," answered Dick. "They'd be too scared. As yet, flying machines are hardly built for ladies. But I think the time will come when they will use them."

As they were in no hurry, the boys took their time in sailing over the farms and country roads. They did not go up very high, and often saw farmers and others staring at them, shouting things they could not catch.

"By and by flying machines will be as common as autos," remarked Dick. "But now the sight of one is a great curiosity to these folks."

Sam handled the machine like a veteran and even showed what he could do by making a small figure eight and a spiral dip.

"I wish we had a little monoplane, just for one," he said. "My! couldn't a fellow scoot around then!"

"Sam's got the flying bee all right!" cried Tom.

"Well, wouldn't you like it yourself?" demanded the youngest Rover.

"I'd rather have a big airship. Then I could give all my friends a ridehave a regular airship party."

"Well, I'd like that too," was Sam's reply.

Presently they came in sight of the seminary buildings. They circled around for some time and then landed at the far end of the campus. A few girls were in sight, but not those they had come to visit.

"Good afternoon," said Dick, to a girl he had met, named Ida Strong. "Can you tell me where I can find Miss Stanhope, or the Misses Laning?"

"The three of them went for a walk, about half an hour ago," replied Ida Strong.

"Do you know where they went?"

"I do not, excepting that they took the road to Beechwood," and the girl student pointed out the highway mentioned, one that ran through the big woods back of the seminary. It led to the village of Beechwood, which was several miles beyond.

"Thank you," returned Dick. "If we shouldn't meet them, will you tell them we called, in our biplane?"

"I will," said the girl.

Dick was about to rejoin his brothers, and suggest that they go up and fly along over the woods road, when another girl, named Bess Haven, came running up.

"Oh, Mr. Rover, isn't this queer!" she cried. "I thought you were hurt!"

"Hurt?" repeated Dick, puzzled. "How so?"

"Why Dora Stanhope said you werethat you had had a fall out of the flying machine."

"That I fell out of the machine?" cried Dick. "There is some mistake here. I have had no fall. When did she tell you that?"

"About half an hour ago. She got some sort of a message, and she was terribly upset. She went off to visit you."

"Where to?"

"I don't know. But waityes, she did say you had had a fall in the woods."

"Did she go alone?" And now Dick's heart began to thump strangely. He was thinking of their many enemies. Was this some new trick?

"No, Nellie and Grace Laning, her cousins, went with her."

Dick turned to Ida Strong.

"You saw them go?"

"Yes, just as I told you. Oh, Mr. Rover, is anything wrong?"

"I don't knowI hope not. But I think we had better go after them at once. Good day." And Dick fairly ran back to where Tom and Sam rested near the biplane.

"Start her up, quick!" he said to his brothers, in a low voice. "Something is wrong! We've got to get after the girls right away!"

"What is it?" demanded Tom, leaping to his feet, while Sam did the same.

"I'll tell you when we are on the way. Quick, start the propellers! I'll take the wheel," and Dick sprang into the seat.

In another moment the engine had been started, and with a rush and a whizz the Dartaway left the campus. Dick made a turn, then headed in the direction of the road through the woods. He flew low and rather slowly.

125

"Keep your eyes open," he cautioned, "for any sight of the girlsor any sight of our enemies." And then he related as much as he knew of what had occurred.

"Do you think somebody sent that message to decoy Dora away from the seminary, Dick?" asked Sam.

"Doesn't it look that way? Why should anybody send word that I was hurt, when I wasn't?"

"I think you are right!" declared Tom. "I think I can see through it," he went on quickly. "They found out they couldn't dynamite dad or Uncle Randolph into giving up that money, and they couldn't get at Mrs. Stanhope or Mrs. Laning to get it, so now they are going to see what they can do through Doraand maybe Nellie and Grace."

"That's exactly the way I figure it!" exclaimed Dick. "And the sooner we reach the girls the better! For all we know, it may even now be too late!"

"Oh, let us hope not!" cried Sam.

"Did they go on foot?" asked Tom.

"Yes."

"Were they to meet anybody?"

"I don't know. Miss Haven said they went off in a great hurrywhich was natural, if they thought I had tumbled out of the biplane and been hurt. I suppose poor Dora was scared half to death," and Dick heaved a long sigh.

As the flying machine swept along over the woods and the roadway the three youths kept their eyes on the alert for a sight of the girls. For a long time they saw nothing out of the ordinary. Then Sam uttered a cry:

"See! see! There is Grace! She is waving her handkerchief at us!"

All looked in the direction indicated, and at a spot along the road where there was quite a cleared space they saw Grace Laning standing on a flat rock, waving frantically at them. They had to make a circle, and then, with care, Dick brought the biplane down into the roadway.

126

"What is it, Grace?" yelled Sam, as he leaped from his seat. "Where are the others?"

"Oh, Sam!" moaned the girl, and then they saw that her hair was awry and her shoes were covered with dust. "Oh, save them! Go after them at once!" And then she staggered forward and fainted in Sam's arms.

The three Rovers were greatly alarmed and for the moment did not know what to do. Then Dick rushed to the side of the roadway, where some water trickled along in a hollow, and brought some, using a collapsible cup they carried when on a trip. With this they bathed Grace's face and they forced a little water into her mouth, and soon she opened her eyes and stared around her.

"Go away! Go away! Don't touch me!" she gasped.

"Hush, Grace, you are safe," answered Sam, gently.

"Oh, Sam! I forgot!" She struggled to her feet, he still supporting her. "Diddid you find them? Did you bring them back?" she asked wildly.

"You mean Dora and Nellie?" asked Dick and Tom, in a breath.

"Yes! yes!"

"We don't know where they are. Tell us about it," went on Dick.

"Oh, it's terrible!" cried Grace, and now the tears began to course down her cheeks. "We got a noteat least Dora didstating you had had a fall from the biplane and were hurt. The note was signed 'Tom,' and we of course thought Tom had sent it. It said to keep the matter quiet but to come without delaydown this road to the old white cottage. So the three of us started off as soon as we could. Dora was so afraid it was serious she ran nearly all the way, and Nellie and I ran, too. We had thought you were at the cottage, but when we got there we didn't see anybody. While we hunted around a big touring car, one of the kind with a closed coach top, dashed up. There was a man running the car and another man inside, a fellow who looked like a doctor. The driver asked if we were the girls who had come to see Dick Rover, the aviator, and we said yes. Then he said the car had been sent for us and for the doctor, and for us to get in and he would take us to Dick Rover at once. We got in, and then, before we knew it, the touring car was rushing along the road at a great rate of speed. We asked the doctor about you, Dick, but he said he hadn't seen you yet. Then we asked the driver, but he acted so queer we began to get suspicious. Then, oh, wasn't it strange? Nellie saw a card on the floor of the car, and picked it up, and it was Josiah Crabtree's visiting card! She showed it to Dora and I, and

Dora screamed, and wanted to leap out of the car. But the doctorif he was a doctorheld her, and held Nellie, too. But I was too much for him. I don't know how I did it, but, just as we were rounding a curve rather slowly, I flung myself out of the door, and I landed in some bushes. I got scratched a little, as you can see, but I wasn't hurt, and I started to run back to the seminary and was doing that when I saw your flying machine. You know the rest." And now Grace stopped, too exhausted to say another word.

"And the touring car went on?" queried Dick.

"Yes! yes! I saw the man shut the door, too. Oh, Dick, they have carried poor Nellie and Dora off, just as they carried Dora's mother off!"

"They kept to this road?"

"I believe so. I don't know of any cross road this side of Beechwood."

"Then we'll get after them at once!" declared Dick. "Sam, do you want to take Grace back, or come with us?"

"WellIer"

"Go with them, Samthey may need you!" broke in the girl quickly. "I can go back alone, and I'll send word to the authorities, over the telephone. Hurry! hurry, or it will be too late!"

The boys needed no further urging. Dick and Tom ran for the flying machine, and soon the explosions of the motor filled the crisp autumn air. Then all the boys leaped on board. Dick was at the wheel, and he sent the Dartaway along at a good rate of speed. Sam looked back, to see Grace hurrying in the direction of Hope Seminary.

"I hope she gets back safely," he said anxiously.

"I think she will," answered Tom. "Those rascals are all further along the roadwaiting for Nellie and Dora."

"Keep your eyes open," put in Dick. "Don't let anything escape you. We must spot that auto without fail!"

Milton Keynes UK
Ingram Content Group UK Ltd.
UKHW010703260923
429409UK00004B/377

9 791041 952564